BLACK LIMIT

CHARLOTTE BYRD

BLACK EDGE SERIES READING ORDER

ABOUT BLACK LIMIT

*I*s this the end of us?

I found a woman I can't live without.

We've been through so much. We've had our set backs. But our love is stronger than ever.

We are survivors.

But when they take her from me at the altar, right before she is to become my wife, everything breaks.

I will do anything to free her. **I will do anything to make her mine for good.**

But is that enough? And what if it's not?

PRAISE FOR BLACK EDGE SERIES

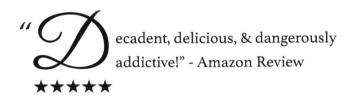 "Decadent, delicious, & dangerously addictive!" - Amazon Review

★★★★★

"TITILLATION SO MASTERFULLY WOVEN, no reader can resist its pull. A MUST-BUY!" - Bobbi Koe, Amazon Review ★★★★★

"CAPTIVATING!" - Crystal Jones, Amazon Review

★★★★★

"EXCITING, INTENSE, SENSUAL" - Rock, Amazon Reviewer ★★★★★

"SEXY, SECRETIVE, PULSATING CHEMISTRY..." - Mrs. K, Amazon Reviewer ★★★★★

"CHARLOTTE BYRD IS A BRILLIANT WRITER. I've read loads and I've laughed and cried. She writes a balanced book with brilliant characters. Well done!" -Amazon Review ★★★★★

"FAST-PACED, DARK, ADDICTIVE, AND COMPELLING" - Amazon Reviewer ★★★★★

"HOT, STEAMY, AND A GREAT STORYLINE." - Christine Reese ★★★★★

"MY OH MY....CHARLOTTE has made me a fan for life." - JJ, Amazon Reviewer ★★★★★

"THE TENSION and chemistry is at five alarm level." - Sharon, Amazon reviewer ★★★★★

"HOT, sexy, intriguing journey of Elli and Mr. Aiden Black. - Robin Langelier ★★★★★

"WOW. Just wow. Charlotte Byrd leaves me speechless and humble... It definitely kept me on the edge of my seat. Once you pick it up, you won't put it down." - Amazon Review ★★★★★

"SEXY, STEAMY AND CAPTIVATING!" - Charmaine, Amazon Reviewer ★★★★★

" INTRIGUE, lust, and great characters...what more could you ask for?!" - Dragonfly Lady ★★★★★

"AN AWESOME BOOK. Extremely entertaining, captivating and interesting sexy read. I could not put it down." - Kim F, Amazon Reviewer ★★★★★

"JUST THE ABSOLUTE BEST STORY. Everything I like to read about and more. Such a great story I will read again and again. A keeper!!" - Wendy Ballard

★★★★★

"IT HAD the perfect amount of twists and turns. I instantaneously bonded with the heroine and of course Mr. Black. YUM. It's sexy, it's sassy, it's steamy. It's everything." - Khardine Gray, Bestselling Romance Author ★★★★★

CHAPTER 1 - ELLIE

*T*he sounds of his voice sends shivers through my body.

What is he doing in my apartment?

Did he follow me here?

He just attacked Aiden and now he's coming for me.

But what can I do?

Stay calm, Ellie, I say to myself. Just stay calm.

"What are you doing here, Blake?" I ask.

"I just wanted to come see you. You know, for old times sake," he says.

When I turn around, I come face-to-face with a disheveled man on the brink of collapse.

His hair is out of control and so are his clothes.

His eyes look frantic and terrified, yet mean all at the same time. He is pointing a gun at me.

"We don't have any old times sake to share, Blake," I say. I stand back, leaning against the kitchen counter. I don't know what to do, but I need to come up with a plan. Fast.

"Aren't you curious how I got here?" he asks, waving the gun around in his hand.

I shrug. I don't know whether it's best to agree with him or to argue.

"What are you doing here, Blake?" I repeat my original question.

"I heard that the cops are looking for me. You know, for shooting Aiden. How is he again?"

His question pierces me through my heart. How dare he ask me about Aiden? How dare he say his name at all?

And then, all out of the blue, I have an idea.

My purse is the crossover kind and it's draped behind me. I turn away from him slightly so that he can't see what I'm doing from behind the kitchen island. When I'm certain that he can't see me, I reach in and bury my hand inside. I search for my phone.

"He's fine," I say. "No thanks to you." I say these words, but my thoughts go back to my phone and the task at hand. All I need to do is remember how to turn the recorder on. I just looked it up a few days ago. I thought it might be a good idea to record my outline for my writing rather than typing it out. Okay, now, try to remember, Ellie. You did it before. What buttons did you press?

"Oh, c'mon," Blake says, taking a few steps toward me. "You're not really mad about that."

To record, I have to open the Voice Memos app. I try to remember where it was visually on the screen because I can't exactly look down and find it without him noticing.

"You don't think I should be?" I ask.

Blake turns away from me. Quickly, I look down at my phone and press on the App Store button. Then I search for Voice Memo and press open.

"How did you get in here?" I ask, pressing on the big red button to record. Just as I drop the phone back into my purse and press my hands on the island for him to see them, Blake says, "Oh, you know, it's amazing what you can find on YouTube these days."

"What do you mean?"

He shrugs. "One of your nice neighbors let me in when I told them that I forgot my key and then I picked your lock."

"You picked my lock? How?"

"I watched a few YouTube videos. Not all of them are useful, you know. Some are total crap."

I take a deep breath. I have no idea what's going to happen, but at least I'm recording it. Now, I need to think of a way out of this.

"You shot Aiden," I say. "Didn't you?"

"Of course, I did," Blake says nonchalantly. "I mean, who the hell do you think shot him?"

My heart sinks to the bottom of my stomach. The way he just admitted that. There's a desperation in his voice. And that's never a good thing to hear.

"I can't believe you just said that," I say before I get a chance to catch myself.

"It's the end, Ellie. There's no reason to lie at the end."

My hands grow cold when I hear that. No. This is not the end for me. I need to do something. I need to save myself and my baby. No matter what.

"The cops are going to be here any minute," I finally say.

"No, they're not. They have no idea that I'm here. They're looking for me, but they don't know where I could be."

He's right, of course. Shit. Okay, think, Ellie. Think.

"There's no point, Ellie," Blake says as if he can read my mind. "There's nothing you can do."

No, he's wrong, I say to myself. He didn't think I could record this whole conversation and here I am doing it. No, there's a lot I can do. I just have to think of it first. And while I do, I have to make him talk.

"Can I ask you something, Blake? What happened between you and Aiden?"

Blake turns around. The expression on his face tells me that he never expected that question, but he's pleasantly surprised.

"I'm going to tell you the truth," he says after a moment. "I mean, nothing else really matters now, right?"

I wait.

"I've always been jealous of Aiden. He was one of my closest friends at Yale. And I always loved him. But he had things easier than I did. And I hated him for it at the same time."

Okay, I say to myself. Just keep him talking until you figure something out.

"Why?" I ask.

"Well, he wasn't rich like me. My parents had these large, overgrown, ridiculous houses with housekeepers and staff. But the thing is that when you're a little kid, you don't care about any of that. You just want your parents."

"And you didn't have that?"

"Nope. My parents just had each other. They spent all their time traveling and they always left me with grandparents, nannies, or whoever."

"I'm sorry about that," I say. I mean it as a lie but it's not really one. I am actually sorry. It's little shit like this that really throws people off and ruins their childhoods. And then they take their broken childhoods out on other people. Like Aiden and me. Fuck his parents!

"I wanted you from the first time I saw you," Blake says. "At the auction. But of course, Aiden got to you first. And I was his friend so I had to go along with it. Do you know how much I hated that?"

"No, not really," I say.

"Aiden hated his parents. He never thought they loved him, but he didn't know how good he had it. Just like with you. He's such an asshole. What the hell do you see in him, Ellie?"

I shrug. I don't really know how to respond, but luckily he doesn't wait for the answer.

"I was so happy to get his job. I finally got something that I deserved. But then they took that away from me. All because the stock price started to drop. I tried to implement his advertising strategy but I didn't know how. And then you two got together again. So, what it did it all matter?"

He is glossing over big swaths of what had happened between us, but I don't dare bring that up. I'm putting my own plan into motion.

"Blake, please let me go. I'm pregnant. Please. I won't tell anyone that you were here. But please, just let me go."

"You're pregnant?"

"It just happened. It was an accident."

"And you're keeping it?"

"I don't know yet," I lie. I don't really know what answer is going to make all of this worse for me.

"Does Aiden know?"

"Aiden is...dead." The word just escapes my lips all

of a sudden. It's not planned. It just sort of slips out.
Maybe if he thought that Aiden was dead then he
would leave me alone? Maybe then he wouldn't have
anyone to be jealous of?

"Blake, I won't say anything about you being here.
But you have to go. The cops are looking for you. Just
go away. Drive away as far as possible from New York
as you can. Go to Mexico. Start over again on
some beach."

I talk and slowly inch my way toward the utensils
drawer at the center of the island. When he casts his
eyes down to the floor, I act fast. I open the drawer
and grab a knife. But within seconds, Blake is next to
me. He tries to grab the knife out of my hand. We
start to wrestle. As I push back on him, I see that he
left the gun on the kitchen island and I lean against
him and swat the gun away. It flies across the room,
giving me at least some sort of shot at living through
this.

Blake slams my hand onto the counter, knocking the
knife out of it. Then he presses his hands around my
throat and starts to squeeze. My airway is completely
blocked. I can't breathe in or out. I don't have much
time. My hands are free and I feel around for

something to grab. When I find it, I wrap my fingers around it and plunge it into his throat. Blood squirts everywhere, covering my face with a thick gooey substance. He lets go of my throat and I collapse onto the floor. It takes me a few moments to catch my breath. When I finally do, I hear a scary gurgling sound coming from somewhere nearby. I throw up and everything turns to black.

CHAPTER 2 - ELLIE

I wake up in a hospital bed with bright lights above me.

"You're awake," Brie says, leaning over me. "You're okay."

I nod, trying to understand where I am. Brie briefs me. Blake had picked a lock to my apartment. I had stabbed him in the neck with a ballpoint pen. He had bled out while I threw up and passed out next to him. A next door neighbor had heard the commotion and called the police. When they got there, they found us and listened to the recording that I had made with my phone. All of this seems about right.

"How's Aiden?" I ask.

Brie helps me up and shows me to his room, which is five stories up. I sit next to him on the bed and take his hand in mine.

"Everything's going to be okay now, honey," I whisper with tears running down my face. "I love you."

CHAPTER 3 - AIDEN

WHEN SHE'S ALL I DREAM ABOUT…

I hear her talking. Her voice sweet and sensual, reminding me of home. She's here. Her presence is undeniable. And yet, she is also far away. Drifting. Fighting to get to me, but being held back by something that's bigger than both of us.

I feel her outstretched arms pulling toward me. I try to lift my hand, but it's all to no avail. I try to lift my hand, but I can't. It's like I have something large and incredibly heavy pressing down on my chest, making it impossible for me to move even an inch.

"Ellie!" I yell on top of my lungs, but don't hear a single sound come out. I don't have a voice.

"Ellie! Ellie!" I try again. But again, nothing comes out. She is yearning for me, tears are running down her face, but she can't hear me. It's like we are separated by one of those two-way mirrors in police stations. I can see her, but she can't see me. I can hear her, but she can't hear me.

I don't want to give up. I don't have a choice. I lie back down in bed, leaning against the tough hospital pillows, and watch her. Her hair cascades around her shoulders. Her face is puffy with tears. Her eyelashes, waterlogged with droplets, frame her almond-shaped eyes, which are wise beyond their years. She's holding my hand. Her nails are brittle and bitten down, a sign of nervousness. Hair is falling into her face and I would do anything to get up and push it away. I would give anything to touch her cheek again, press it against mine, and tell her that everything is going to be okay.

Somewhere in the distance, doctors gather around to discuss me. Tears run down Ellie's face and she buries it in her hands. One of the doctors, the younger one, puts his hand around her shoulders to comfort her. What did they tell her? Why can't I hear them? Why can't I move?

My mind starts to drift. I try to remember how I got here in the first place. My memory is blurry. I remember only bits and pieces. The flashing lights of the emergency vehicle. The hurrying men and women in uniform who gather around me. All the equipment beeping around me as they put me onto a stretcher and drive off. The bright lights of the operating room. More people milling around. Everyone talking at me, but not to me. Someone saying, "Is that really him? Aiden Black?"

But earlier than that? What of those memories? There's Ellie tied to a post on my yacht. The most beautiful woman I've ever seen. I craved her ever since the first moment that I saw her. There's Ellie swimming in the turquoise Caribbean waters in her bikini. Her wide hips and gorgeous breasts, like two temples, moving like molasses up and down as she runs toward me. For once, she isn't wearing a cover-up and covering up every one of her delicious curves.

There's walking with Ellie hand in hand through the woods in Maine. The smell of falling leaves drenched in November rain. Her fingers were freezing, looking for warmth in mine. Things changed for us that night. Life came at us at full force and tried to knock us off our course. But it didn't.

What else do I remember? The way her hair smells of lavender, and hope, and summer. When she smiles at me, I know that nothing bad can ever happen and even if it does, we will be okay, no matter what. Like now? Right? She's not standing far away from me, but I can't reach her. She's crying and she can't stop. She's choking on her tears. They're coming faster and faster. She can barely keep up. I want to touch her. Put my arm around her. Tell her that it's all going to be okay. But there's a thick curtain separating us. It's not real; it's all in my head. Or maybe it's not. I don't really know.

"Ellie!" I try again. "Ellie!"

I yell her name over and over until my throat is parched and dry. But she can't hear me. No one can. I'm all alone. Unreachable.

CHAPTER 4 - ELLIE

WHEN EVERYTHING'S NOT OKAY...

*E*verything is supposed to be okay. Blake is gone and I'm okay. Badly shaken and somewhat hurt, but not really with any scars that will last too long. And yet, everything is wrong. Aiden is here, alive, but not really. I see him lying in the hospital bed and he's not really present. He's breathing. It looks like he's sleeping, but he is far away from me. The doctors don't know what's wrong. They have put him into a medically-induced coma. They are debating as to when they should take him out. The older doctor thinks that the sooner they take him out, the better. The younger ones aren't so sure. They think his body needs time to rest. Recover. None of them know what he will be like when they eventually take him out. I can see fear in their eyes. They aren't saying it, but they are huddling around, whispering. They don't want to tell me the truth. My heart is sinking. I wait and wait and as more and more time passes, the less hope I have.

"Everything's going to be okay now, honey," I whisper with tears running down my face. I'm holding his hand. I can feel him here with me. His body is frail. His face is alabaster white. His long eyelashes and hair have lost their luster. His skin is dry in patches and I apply moisturizer, but it doesn't do much. The harshness of the hospital lights makes everything worse. More bleak.

I tell Aiden that everything's going to be okay over and over again until I believe it myself.

"Ellie." Brie comes over and puts her hand on mine. I look up at her.

"You've been sitting here all day. Maybe you should get out. Get some fresh air."

I shrug. Maybe, but that's not exactly what I want to do. I shake my head.

"No, I can't. I want to stay here. With him."

"I know you do, but he's...asleep."

That's an unusual turn of phrase. Neither of us wants to say that Aiden is in a coma. It sounds so medical. So surreal. Unreal. Like something that only happens in fictional stories. This is real life. Real people don't go into comas, right? They aren't put into comas, right? Wrong. Of course.

I look at Aiden. He looks tired and worn out and asleep. But then...a movement!

"Oh my God!" I say, grabbing Brie's hand. "Oh my God! He's moving!"

I press the call button on his bed. "He's moving, Brie! He's moving!"

Brie leans over me. We both watch his face. His eyes are moving under his eyelids. His fingers give mine a squeeze. One squeeze. Then another and another.

"Aiden, Aiden. Can you hear me?" I whisper, wiping the tears running down the outside of my cheek.

"You're going to be okay, honey. I'm here for you." I press the call button over and over again. "Where's the nurse? Why isn't she coming?"

"I'm going to go find one," Brie says, running out of the room. When she returns a few minutes later, she brings not only the nurse, but also two students and one of Aiden's younger doctors. Dr. Briggs.

I move out of the way as they hover around Aiden's bed. They take his vitals and check the equipment.

"What's happening?" I ask eagerly. My heartbeat is going so fast, it feels like my heart is about to burst out of my chest. I clench my fists in anticipation. The jagged edges of my nails dig into the palms of my hands.

"I'm sorry, Ellie," Dr. Briggs says after a moment with a sullen expression on her face. She's not meeting my gaze, casting her eyes at the floor instead. "What you saw there is something that is pretty common in coma patients. They look like they're waking up, but in fact it's just an involuntary reaction. They are alive and their neurons are just firing, making them have these movements."

"No, no, no." I shake my head. More tears flow down my face, only these are tears of anger and sadness instead of hope. Brie wraps her arms around me. Dr. Briggs continues to talk, to explain more and more about Aiden's condition. But she's not so much talking to me as to the nurse and the students. I can't bear to listen. I bury my head in Brie's arms and cry.

When I finally come up for air, everyone is gone. It's just Brie, Aiden, and me once again.

"I'm going to get some coffee," she says. "Are you going to be okay?"

I nod and ask her to bring me a cup of hot tea.

"I love you, Aiden," I say when we are all alone. "I'm going to be here no matter what. Until you come out of this coma."

His eyelids move again, giving me only a glimmer of hope. At least, he's still alive. At least, he's still there.

"Come back to me, Aiden," I whisper. "Come back to me."

———

HOURS PASS AND DARKNESS FALLS. I don't even bother looking at the time anymore. Brie goes home, but I stay. I pull the chair closer to Aiden's bed and recline. It technically unfolds into something

resembling a couch, but I don't have the energy to
deal with it. Instead, I curl up and watch something
stupid on my phone. When my eyes grow tired, I put
on an audiobook. *Outlander*. The narrator's soothing
voice with the beautiful English accent lulls me into
a state of serenity. The faraway land with all of its
foreign conventions and old fashioned traditions
allows me to drift away, escape from reality.

I see him. His cocky grin. His unforgiving eyes. He's
trying to grab for my knife. He's overpowering me.
He's stronger than I am; I feel my life slipping away.
Everything flashes before my eyes. My parents
playing with me in a baby pool. Walking down the
aisle at my mom's wedding. Visiting my dad at his
house and watching game shows silently in the dark.
Standing before everyone at the auction. Feeling
Aiden's gaze on me. Feeling his warm body next to
mine. Watching him reach the heights of ecstasy as
he plunges deep inside of me. Then, there's Blake
again. He's on top of me, overpowering me. I kick his
gun away. He slams my hand onto the counter.
Shooting pains run up and down my arm. And then,
he wraps his strong hands around my neck. Choking
me. I can't breathe. My arms flail around, looking for

a way out. Darkness is descending and all I see is Aiden before me, asking me to marry him.

No, no, no, I hear myself yelling. Light is disappearing around me, but I have to fight on. I have to prevail. My breaths are becoming more arduous. I keep trying to inhale but no air gets in. I'm wheezing as Blake's hands get a firmer grip around my throat. My eyes start to feel like they're about to bulge out of my head. Everything starts to feel fuzzy and far away. My life is slowly draining out of me. But my fingers continue their search. There has to be a way out of this. Finally, I stumble upon a possibility. Something smooth, but hard, also long. I wrap the fingers of my right hand firmly around the object and, with one swift motion, bring it up to his face. I plunge it into his neck. Warm blood rushes out, covering my face. And finally, his strong grip around my neck relaxes. But I don't give up. I don't have another chance. I wrap my fingers even tighter around the object. It's slippery now and I feel like I'm about to lose it. This time around, I plunge it even deeper. Blood splatters everywhere and he falls to the floor. Gasping for breath, I wake up.

CHAPTER 5 - ELLIE

WHEN SHE SHOWS UP…

*T*wo days later, nothing much is different. The doctors come around, check on his progress, note that he's not really making any, and leave. Nurses and nursing assistants come around to check on his vitals and write down what the printouts from all the beeping monitors say. Brie stays with me until she gets bored and then wanders around the hallways looking for something to do. But I stay put. I don't really know what else to do. I don't want to go home. It's still a crime scene. And I'm afraid of being there. I can't go to my mom's house. It's too far and too sad. So, instead, I park myself in his room and wait. And wait. And then I wait some more.

A detective comes to speak to me about what happened with Blake. He listens, scribbles notes down in his little book, then comes back later that day with more questions. The neighbors corroborate my story. So far, they are not interested in pressing charges. But they will be doing more investigating.

"You can go back home," he says when he's about to leave. "It's no longer an active crime scene."

I nod as if any of that makes sense. My home - an active crime scene. I don't want to go back, so Brie goes alone. She comes back with my laptop, a notebook, and some clothes. I look through the stuff she had brought. There's a pair of jeans, but that seems to be too ambitious of an undertaking. Luckily, there are also two pairs of yoga pants and some loose-fitting t-shirts and a hoodie. Perfect. I won't need anything else. Except maybe some makeup so I don't look like I'm half-dead. That's a bad joke to make in a hospital. I know that. So, I keep it to myself.

When Brie goes out to the movies, I sit down next to Aiden and open my laptop. I need to write. When I have no energy at all, I listen to audiobooks to escape. When I have some energy, but not enough to sustain myself entirely, I read to escape. But right now, I feel a ball forming in the pit of my stomach. It's an energy that needs to be expelled, one way or another. The best way to get rid of it is to write. I open a blank document and start typing. It starts with an emotion. I describe how much I hate Blake and how much I love Aiden. But these words quickly morph into a story. I type until my fingers start to ache and my wrists develop a dull shooting pain going back to my elbows. I've always been susceptible to carpal tunnel, but typically it takes longer than just a few thousand words for it to feel this bad.

I shake my head as I close my laptop. It's Blake's fault. Yet another thing that he has caused.
Fuck him!

"Excuse me," an unfamiliar female voice says. I look up and see a woman with dark hair, which is cut bluntly at the shoulders. She has high cheekbones and tired eyes. I've never met her before, but the resemblance is uncanny.

"Oh, Aiden." She runs over and grabs his hand. I get

out of my chair to make room. Tears run down her cheeks as she kisses his hand over and over again. Suddenly, I start to feel queasy again. The nausea is far from gone, even though the medication is helping. But anytime I feel at all upset, or over-stimulated, I start to feel nauseated again. I move over to the sofa and sit down.

"I'm so sorry," she mumbles, half looking over at me, but mostly touching Aiden as if she's making sure that he's real.

It takes her a few minutes to fully gather herself. When she finally does, she looks over at me. Her cheeks are still wet and her lips are puffy from the avalanche of tears.

"Hi, I'm Ellie," I whisper, extending my hand. She pulls me close to her, giving me a big warm hug. I exhale deeply, letting myself relax into her.

"Hi, sweetie," she says. "I'm Arlene Black, Aiden's mother."

The last bit isn't necessary. Anyone who knows Aiden would know that she's his mother immediately. They have the same far-off stare, the same large eyes, and chiseled jaw. That's not to imply that she is at all manly. No, she's actually quite feminine.

"I'm so sorry that we have to meet under these circumstances," she says, sitting down next to me. I don't know what I was expecting, but Arlene Black is quite ordinary. She's average weight and height and she's dressed in a casual pair of black pants, boots, and a white blouse. I try to remember what Aiden said she did for a living, but nothing comes to mind.

"Did you talk to the doctors, Mrs. Black?" I ask.

"Oh, please, call me Arlene," she says. "Yes, I did. Do you think they know what they're doing?"

I shrug. "I have no idea."

"I'm going to look into this a little more once I get a hold of myself a bit. I just found out."

"I'm so sorry I didn't call you. It's just that...I didn't know any of your information."

The truth is that it hadn't really occurred to me to call her. Aiden mentioned her only once to me. But I also would have no clue as to how to go about trying to find her. I was too wrapped up in my own grief to give calling his relatives and letting them know about this any thought.

"The police reached out to me. They said that Blake attacked him."

"Yes."

"I've always had a bad feeling about him. Even when they were first getting friendly at Yale," Arlene says, shaking her head.

I doubt that it was that obvious, but we all have to say things to ourselves to make us feel better.

"He attacked you as well?"

I nod. That word, attacked, sends shivers through my body. Suddenly, a flashback. I see Blake's face before me. I try to breathe but choke up.

"Oh, sweetie, I'm so sorry, I didn't mean to..." her voice trails off as she hands me a cup of water. As soon as an ice cube touches the tip of my tongue, the memory of Blake vanishes and I find myself back in the hospital room.

"No, I'm sorry. It's all very...fresh, still."

She nods and sits back down next to Aiden. I make

myself comfortable next to her. Neither of us speak for some time. The silence is comforting actually. I let my thoughts drift and, for a while, I hear nothing but the beeping of the machines.

"So, how did you two meet?"

CHAPTER 6 - ELLIE

WHEN WE GET TO KNOW EACH OTHER…

*W*ith that one question, Arlene shatters the quiet and brings me back to reality. How did we meet? Well, actually, I auctioned myself off to the highest bidder at a private auction that your son hosted on his yacht. He ended up paying the highest price and then he did bad things to me. Really bad things that I really loved. This is not exactly the kind of truth that a mother wants to hear. I want to lie. But I can't. What if she knows the truth? Our relationship hasn't exactly been kept out of the gossip papers.

"We met on his yacht," I say. It's not a lie, but it's not exactly the whole truth either.

"It's beautiful, isn't it?" Arlene asks. I nod and smile.

"It's still hard to believe that my son can afford something like that. He didn't exactly grow up in the lap of luxury."

"Very few people are as wealthy as he is," I say after a moment. "You must be very proud."

She shrugs. "I always wanted him to pursue his passion, but I never cared much about money. He gets that from his father."

"What does his father do?" I ask.

"He's a sanitation worker. Garbage man."

"Oh, okay." I nod.

Sensing that I'm somewhat confused by her statements, she explains. "Dean, my husband, was... is...a dreamer. He worked in sanitation all of his life but that didn't stop him from thinking up a million different ways to make money. When he isn't drinking, he's scheming. There's always that perfect business idea just around the corner."

I don't really know how to respond to this except to nod along.

"Aiden is a lot like Dean. When he was a kid, he was

always starting businesses. A lemonade stand. A snow removal business, even though he didn't even own a shovel. He borrowed ours, broke it, and then got a loan from one of his customers to buy another one. The difference between Aiden and his father is that he has dedication and follow through. And a good, very good, work ethic."

"Yeah, Aiden is a hard worker."

"Dean and I are going through a divorce. I don't know if Aiden told you. We have been separated for years."

"No, he didn't."

In fact, come to think of it, Aiden has told me very little about his family. Up until this moment, I didn't even know what his mom's name was.

"I'm sorry about that," I add.

"Don't be. Dean and I have had a very complicated relationship for many years. He's an alcoholic, you know."

I nod. No, I didn't know. And I don't really know how to respond to this statement either. I have never met Aiden's dad and have nothing really to contribute to the conversation except for more questions.

"So, Aiden said he grew up in Boston?"

"Yep, Waltham. It's not too far from there."

"So, what did you do for a living?" I ask. Oh, shit. That's a loaded question. What if she was a homemaker? I didn't mean to make her feel bad.

"Did? I still do. I'm a nurse."

"Oh, okay." I let out a sigh of relief. "I just thought since Aiden is so...wealthy that you wouldn't have to work anymore."

"I don't, but I enjoy what I do. I worked as a nurse for many years. I no longer work at a hospital, but I can't very well just sit around all day like Dean drinking myself to death. I teach nursing now."

"Oh, that's interesting."

Brie can't come back soon enough. I'm growing exhausted talking to her and I still feel quite queasy. Suddenly, I feel so sick to my stomach that I have to excuse myself and run to the bathroom.

"So, how far along are you?" Arlene asks, much to my surprise. I stare at her, dumbfounded.

"Um, twelve weeks," I mumble. "How did you...?"

"Like I said, I'm a nurse. A very good one. Your face is flushed, your breasts look tender, and you just ran to the bathroom to throw up. It doesn't take a detective."

I rub my eyes and run my hands through my hair.

"We're not really telling anyone," I say after a moment. "I mean...that's why Aiden didn't tell you."

"No." Arlene shakes her head. "Aiden didn't tell me because he hates me. I doubt that he would've even told me at all if he wasn't lying here in a coma."

I look away. I want to desperately know why he hates her, but this doesn't seem like the right moment. She just found out that she will be having a grandchild. I want her to enjoy it instead of focusing on why her child dislikes her so much that he had kept it a secret from her.

"I'm very happy for you both," she says after a moment.

"Thank you. It was a surprise."

"From the deer in headlights look on your face, I'd say so."

To say that Arlene has a jagged edge to her would be an understatement. If this is how she is with practically a stranger, I can only imagine how she is at home. I don't necessarily dislike her, she's just putting me on guard.

"It's going to be okay, you know," Arlene says after a moment. "You're going to find out that you're actually capable of being a mother. And a good one at that."

"Wow, thank you," I say, taken a little aback by her generosity. "I really appreciate it."

"I wasn't the best mother, but I tried my best. Children are always disappointed. The least you can do is to give it your all."

CHAPTER 7 - ELLIE

I don't exactly know what to do with all the information that Arlene states, so I just zone out a little and nod along. She is definitely the teacher type, a kind of person who loves to give out advice, regardless of whether anyone is listening to her or not.

"So, what was Aiden like when he was little?"

"Sweet boy. Very sweet, indeed. But also kind of a recluse. He had a hard time making friends."

I nod. Who doesn't?

"He spent all of his time with computers. He loved to read science fiction and fantasy, watch Star

Wars and Lord of the Rings, all the usual lore. But he wasn't a nerd in the traditional sense. He wasn't a big fanboy, someone who goes to the comic book conventions, places like that. So he didn't make a lot of friends with kids with similar interests."

There's something about her manner of speaking. It's like she's there, but she's not. Detached. A psychologist giving an opinion about a patient to a colleague.

"When he got older, he became withdrawn, private. Even more closed off."

Suddenly, I get the overwhelming urge to slap her. She is sitting here talking about her son, my fiancé, as if he's not here. As if he can't hear her.

"He seems to have gotten over his issues with people," I defend him. "I mean, he did start Owl."

"A tech company? Places like that only foster his kind of isolation."

"I'm not sure what you're trying to say, Arlene."

"That my son has some challenges when it comes to people," she says with an incensed expression on her face. "I mean, you are the one who asked about him as a child."

I don't know what Aiden's particular issue is with his mother. All I know is that I dislike her. A lot. Her judgments and her dismissive attitude, it just makes me want to tell her to go to hell.

Just then, someone bursts through the door. He runs over to Aiden and plops his whole body on top of his. Arlene turns around to face the window in disgust. The man is about her age with a significant bald spot. He has a protruding beer belly that makes him resemble a grizzly as he maneuvers around.

He keeps calling Aiden's name over and over again, much to Arlene's annoyance.

"Ellie, this is Dean, Aiden's father."

I mumble a polite hello. This doesn't seem to be the right moment for anything else. Eventually, Dean pulls himself away from Aiden and looks at me.

"You're goin' to be a grandfather, Dean," Arlene says as a matter of fact. Now, I seriously want to punch her in her stupid face. Who the hell does she think she is? Just because she figured something out about me, and I was stupid enough to reveal it, does not mean she has the right to blabber it to just anyone.

"Really? Oh, wow!" Dean walks over to me and gives me a big warm hug. There is genuine affection emanating from him in addition to a strong odor of booze.

The three of us stand around looking at Aiden for a few moments. None of us would be here were it not for him and he's lying there, listlessly. Asleep. For who knows how long?

Brie comes in with a few doctors who again gather at the far end of the room to discuss the situation before telling any of us anything. I make brief introductions and then sit back down on the sofa. There have been way too many social interactions for me for one day. Exhausted, emotionally drained, and sick from being pregnant is not the best way to meet your fiancé's parents. Perhaps, I wouldn't have had as much contempt toward Arlene if I had met her under other circumstances. But life throws at us what life throws at us, I guess.

Finally, the doctors turn around and tell us their opinion. It's a good idea to keep him in the medically-induced coma for some time longer. How long? They don't know. Their big plan is to just monitor the situation and see how it goes. I shake my head. Dean melts into a nearby chair. Arlene narrows her eyes.

"I think we would like a second opinion," she says.

"Yes, of course. You are definitely entitled to it."

Arlene talks out loud about flying out a doctor someone had recommended to her. Or even flying Aiden to a better hospital. Brie and I exchange looks while Dean just looks down at the floor.

"I don't think flying Mr. Black anywhere is a good idea," Dr. Briggs says. "His condition needs to be monitored. It's very precarious. It could make him a lot worse."

"How much worse can he be?" Arlene exclaims. "He's already in a coma."

"Many people successfully come out of medically-induced comas. We just have to monitor him and wait. I know that this is very difficult," Dr. Briggs says. She is polite and composed, but I can tell that Arlene is trying her patience.

"No, no, no. This can't be it. Money is no option. Do you understand that? We can have anyone in the world here."

Dr. Briggs looks at her blankly.

"Are you seriously telling us that you are the best in the world?" Arlene asks, crossing her arms. I feel the need to butt in.

"Arlene, please, they're doing the best they can," I say.

"That's not my concern. They may be doing the best they can, but my son deserves more than this. They think I don't know how medicine works? The reason they're conferring like that in the corner is to come up with one position and to stick with it. Well, this isn't the law. This isn't some hypothetical argument that we're making. We're talking about my son. Aiden Black."

Dr. Briggs continues to respond, trying to convince her that they're doing the right thing. Other doctors and nurses also pipe in. But it's all to no avail. The more they argue, the more insistent and certain she becomes. It has to be her way or the highway.

I still have no idea what it is that happened between her and Aiden, but I'm getting that sense that she was trying to steamroll him the way she has been trying to steamroll his doctors and clearly steamrolled his father. I'm pretty sure that Aiden got fed up with it though. He's not one to be controlled easily.

"What do you think, Ellie?" Arlene asks, turning to me. I shrug and shake my head.

"Honestly, I don't know," I mumble. Arlene narrows her eyes. I'm not taking her side and that's a problem. "But a second opinion couldn't hurt."

"Goddamn right!" she exclaims and gives me a warm hug. "You see. The women who love this man understand."

I feel sick to my stomach and it's not just because I'm pregnant. The truth is that I have no idea what we should do. I want to believe Dr. Briggs and the rest of the doctors, but what if I'm wrong? What if waiting isn't good? What if...

There are so many things that I don't know, can't know. I mean, if the doctors don't know, how are we, mere laymen, expected to make these decisions?

"I think it might be best to have another doctor come out here for a second opinion. Instead of doing something rash like going through all the trouble of moving him," I say.

Brie smiles at me, approvingly. But when I turn to Arlene, I see a completely different expression. She looks pissed. Her face is flushed and her ears look like they are about to have steam coming out of them.

"Let's just see what they have to say," I say to appease her. "I just want what's best for him."

"And you don't think I do?" she barks at me. I bite my lower lip and look away. I'm not good at confrontation or fighting. Actually, I sort of hate it. But that doesn't mean that I'm going to let myself be bullied by her or anyone else. Getting another opinion is the right thing to do. The more doctors who can agree with Dr. Briggs and her team the better it is, especially, since money isn't really a problem here.

Eventually, all of the doctors and nurses leave and the only people that remain are Arlene, Dean, Brie, and me. And, of course, Aiden. I want to ask them all to leave so I can be alone with Aiden again, but it doesn't feel right. Things are already tense enough between Arlene, Dean, and me that I need to do something to smooth this over.

"Aiden's going to be okay," I say, taking his hand. "You're going to be okay, right?"

I want her to put her arm around me. I want her to believe in this, too. It's more true if more people believe in something, right?

"With doctors like these, I'm not so sure," Arlene says.

The next hour passes at a snail's pace. I look at the clock over and over, but it doesn't do much. Brie and I talk about nonsense. News, nothing political, or controversial. Gossip. The weather. I hope that if we chitchat long enough, one of them will finally get the message. Okay, c'mon, it's time for you and Dean to leave, I keep saying silently to myself.

"So, what time will you be coming back tomorrow?" Arlene asks without looking up from her magazine.

"Wait, what?" My heart sinks.

"Tomorrow? You're coming back tomorrow, right?"

"Yes, I'll be here tomorrow. But I'm staying tonight."

"Oh, that won't be necessary," she says dismissively.

I stare at her, dumfounded. "I know it's not necessary. But it's something that I want to do. I want to be here for Aiden."

"Honey, you are pregnant. You need a good night's rest. He'll be here tomorrow. Besides, I'll stay with him."

Her words are sweet and saccharine just like they were when we first met, but it's all bullshit. It's all a facade.

"I'd really like to stay," I say decisively. Two can play at this game. I want to be here for Aiden and she will not drive me away.

"Ellie, please. I haven't seen my son for a long time. I need to be alone with him," she says. I'm taken aback by the frankness. I don't know if it's another tactic or the truth. Either way, I don't really have much of a choice. I feel like I have to go. At least, for tonight.

CHAPTER 8 - ELLIE

"It's going to be okay, honey," Brie says as we walk out of the hospital into an early spring snowstorm. She doesn't know that, but I play along. It's exactly the kind of thing that I need to hear right now. I don't want to take a cab or go into the subway. It's about a half an hour walk from the hospital, but the fresh air feels nice. Even if it is bone-chilling. As we walk, I lean against Brie and let her hold me up.

"I don't want to go inside," I say when we turn onto my street. I hadn't realized how much I was dreading going up there until this very moment.

"It's going to be okay," Brie says, squeezing my shoulders.

I shake my head. Tears roll down my face.

"Do you want to go get a hotel?"

"Yes," I mumble. "No."

She waits for me to make a decision.

"Okay, let's go in," I finally say.

"Are you sure?"

"No, but it's now or never."

————

WALKING INSIDE, I expect to feel him here again. His anger. My fear. I expect to feel plunging that pen into his neck. Red blood running down my arm. I'm surprised when I don't. After the cops took down the crime scene tape and collected all of their evidence, Brie ordered a crime scene cleanup crew to come and make everything normal again. They did a good job. It's so clean now, you can practically eat off the floor. Too clean, actually. It was never like this when Caroline and I were here. I glance over at Caroline's door. She isn't here anymore either. Tears run down my cheeks as Brie walks me to my room and undoes the covers.

"You need to sleep."

My eyes close before Brie leaves the room.

HE'S HERE AGAIN. I can smell the sweetness of his breath. I can feel his hatred for me. His jealousy of Aiden. He's standing over me. You won't get away this time. This time, you're going to pay. I'm going to take what's mine. You belong to me. Aiden is dead. I killed him. And now you will be mine forever.

THE WIND GETS KNOCKED out of my chest. I open my eyes gasping for breath. My head is swimming. I'm drenched in cold sweat. I slowly rise to my feet and stumble to the bathroom. I don't make it to the toilet. I throw up in the sink and then collapse onto the floor.

I DON'T KNOW how much time has passed. My body is shaking from the cold. I'm lying on the tile floor. My hair is wet and it's sticking to the floor. I try to get

up, but my head feels heavy. Impossible to move.
The closest I get is to roll over to my side. No, I can't.
I close my eyes again and drift away.

"ARE YOU OKAY? ELLIE?" Someone is shaking me. My
eyelids are pushing down on me. I'm not strong
enough to open them.

"Ellie!" She shakes me.

"Brie...what are you doing?" I mumble. Every
muscle in my body is stiff. I'm a Tin Man who needs
to oil his joints.

"I got sick during the night," I say. "And then...I fell
asleep?"

"Oh my God, I thought something had happened,"
she gasps. Well, something did technically happen. I
climb to my feet and try to gather my thoughts. That
was not the most pleasant night, to say the least.

Brie helps me to the living room and makes me
some pancakes. I smother mine in maple syrup and
dig in wholeheartedly. The carbs and the sugar
hardly matter now.

Looking around, I get the feel of the place. It looks like my old place. Cleaner, yes. But it's not really that same place at all. There's no Caroline in the room next to mine. Now, there's Brie. An unexpected, but a much welcome guest. And here at the kitchen island, I feel him. This is where he attacked me. This is where I killed him. Will anything be the same again?

———

UNSURE AS TO what to do before heading to the hospital to see Aiden again, I go back to my room and take out my laptop. My writing is my trusty old friend. If I'm stressed, afraid, or unsure, I sit at my computer and bury myself in a story. Somehow other people's problems make my own seem so much less important. Or maybe they just take me away from them for a little bit. We all need an escape, right?

I open the latest story that I've been working on. Unlike my other work, this isn't fiction. It's the truth, only I'm selling it as fiction because I'm not sure anyone would believe me if they knew the truth. In this story, Caroline is still alive. It's nice to visit with her again. I can almost feel her presence.

After all is said and done, we are nothing but dust in the wind. And stories.

Caroline is gone, but she's with me. Her life is with me. And as long as I can write down her story, she will continue to be with me.

I know for a fact that's why people read my books. They escape into them. They take them away from their everyday problems. And for that, I'm grateful.

The doorbell rings. Brie answers and then comes and knocks on my door.

"There's a package here for you."

"I'll be right there." I don't take off my earphones as I continue to frantically type. When words are flowing, I don't dare interrupt. I have to see where they take me. I'm the writer of the story, but I'm on a journey of discovery as much as the reader. Most of the time, I don't have a plan. And even if I do, it's only in the beginning. Then I veer off course and that's where most of the exciting parts of the story come from.

"What's up?"

"This came for you."

I pick up the small gray package and turn it around. No return address. No description on the top. Hmm, odd. I dig into it, but it's a hard plastic that doesn't give much. After a few moments, I give up and grab a pair of scissors from the drawer.

"Oh my God," I whisper, opening the small black box inside the envelope.

"What is it?"

I take them out and lay them carefully on my palm. Brie and I both stare at the delicate drop earrings with a two-tone circle at the bottom. They are strong and rigid in design. The circle at the end is divided into two halves - marble and gold.

The box comes with a little note.

THESE MADE me think of you. I hope you like them.

Love forever,

Aiden

My heart skips a beat. Tears start to run down my cheeks.

"He must've ordered you these before he…" Brie says, her voice dropping off.

I nod and caress the earrings with my fingers. I love them, Aiden. They are perfect. Suddenly, I miss Aiden so much, I double over in pain.

"I need to see him."

CHAPTER 9 - AIDEN

WHEN I'M LYING HERE....

They don't think I can hear them, but I can. Arguing. Fighting. Just like they did when I was growing up. Why they ever got married in the first place, I have no idea. Were they like this before I was born? Or did I make them into these people?

Their voices low, but loud. They are whispering, but they might as well be talking. I can only make out some of the things that they're saying.

"Your fault."

"Bitch."

"Drunk."

I'm back to being nine years old, sitting in my room, listening to my parents fight downstairs. They don't think their voices have the ability to carry upstairs. I never say anything. It's easier for me to pretend that I can't hear. When I get my first set of headphones, I turn the sound up so loud, I actually don't hear them. From then on, I associate loud music with my parents fighting. That doesn't make going to concerts very fun.

Why are they even here? Who invited them? Who told them? I didn't tell Ellie about them on purpose. I wanted to pretend that they didn't exist. I wanted to pretend that I was this solid, adult man with no baggage. But none of us grow up without baggage, do we? Perhaps, the process of growing and maturing is the process of forgiving your parents for what they've done. Forgiving, but not forgetting. None of us forget. We all aim to become better versions of ourselves with our own kids. Was that my parents aim as well?

All of my grandparents died when I was quite young. I don't have any siblings; just these two. They never get tired of saying that they have stayed together all those years before the divorce for me. Well, who the hell asked them to?

My thoughts drift to my own child. Will I come out of this intact enough to be the father that he or she will need? Will Ellie and I ever be a real family? My hatred for Blake has subsided to the recesses of my mind. I do not spend any more of my energy on him. It's not worth it. He did what he did. He got me into this predicament. I don't have any control over the past. All I can do is learn to live with it right now. In the present.

The monitors beep somewhere in the background, but not loud enough to drown out their voices. Ellie's not here now. I can't sense her sweet presence. All I can do is hope that she will come back soon. I need her. I crave her. I don't know where I would be without her.

Dean shuffles his feet as he walks. Arlene stomps her high heels. She uses her fingers to display aggression; he cowers in a corner in return. What have they done to each other over the years? Will Ellie and I ever be like them? No, no, no. Ellie and I are in love. Ellie is my soulmate and I hope that I am hers. We get each other. We are never cruel or hateful. If I ever feel like I'm becoming my parents... I'm going to put an end to it. My child will never hear an ugly word. My child will never hear me disrespect their mother. My child will feel only love coming from me. Children deserve that. It's not something that I ever had, and it's something that I will certainly give my child if I get the chance.

Beep.

Beep.

Beep.

"What are you doing? Stop that."

"You knew about this last night, you wino. Why don't you drink a little less so you can be here a little more for your child?"

"Fuck you!"

"Fuck you!"

"Please, please, Mr. and Mrs. Black. You have to stop fighting. This is having an effect on your son."

"Oh, c'mon. He's a vegetable, can't you see that? He's not here! You all did this to him!"

"Mrs. Black, I'm going to have to ask you to leave."

"I don't care. I've signed the paperwork. I'm taking him to a place where he can get actual help."

"Mrs. Black, please. He's in no condition to be moved. Is his fiancée okay with this?"

"I don't care. Ellie's got no say in this. She's not his wife. She's a nobody."

Beep.

Beep.

Beep.

CHAPTER 10 - ELLIE

I rub my new earrings between my fingers as I sit in the back of a cab. Brie is staring out of the window with a pensive look on her face.

"Are you okay?" She turns to me and asks.

"Yeah." I nod. "Just hope that something is different today."

I run my fingertips over the soft metal at the end of the earring, and suddenly I feel close to him. It's like he's almost right here next to me. My heart skips a beat. I can't wait to see him. To take his hand in mine. To kiss his palms and thank him. Mainly, to tell him that I'm going to be here for him no matter what.

"It's going to be okay," Brie mumbles. I narrow my eyes. Something doesn't feel right.

"What's wrong?" I ask.

She shrugs. "Nothing."

"What?"

"I just have a bad feeling about something. I don't want to worry you."

"About Aiden?"

"Yes."

"Brie…" I plead. Take it back. Why are you telling me this?

"I'm sorry. I shouldn't have said anything. It's not my place."

"No, you shouldn't have. I'm worried enough."

"I know you are," she mumbles.

The cab can't get to the hospital fast enough. While

Brie pays, I run inside and speed over to his room. The anticipation that I had felt earlier somehow morphed into full blown anxiety in a matter of minutes. Brie's premonition has taken over my mind. What if she's right? What if something happened last night? How could I have been so stupid? Why did I leave him alone in that room with his horrible parents?

I run up to the nurses' station on his floor. They are laughing and chatting happily, holding cups of coffee. Then they see me. Their faces drop. My heart sinks.

"What? What happened?" I demand. I run to his room.

"Ellie, please." I hear them behind me.

When I burst through the doors, I see nothing but an empty bed. It has been cleaned. The sheets are made. Perfect hospital corners. It's waiting for its next patient.

"What's going on? Where's Aiden?" My heart seizes up. I can't breathe. I start to see little dots all around my peripheral vision.

"Ellie, please, calm down," one of the nurses says, putting her hand around my shoulder. I knock it off.

"Where's Aiden?!" I scream.

"He's..." the nurse starts to say. I get dizzy. I try to sit down, but I miss the chair behind me and land straight on the cold linoleum floor.

"Oh my God! Ellie!" Brie runs over and helps me up. Somehow the fall knocks me out of this sense of helplessness. The room is no longer closing in on me. I take a few deep breaths and look at the nurse whose name I can't remember.

"Tell me," I say, preparing myself for the worst.

"His parents took him to a hospital in Boston."

I hear her words in my head, but I don't really process them. What? Why? Who the hell gave them that right?

"His mom made the decision last night. She was convinced that the doctors here don't know what they're doing."

"I thought that they were just going to get someone to come in for a second opinion," I say. Dr. Briggs comes into the room with a crestfallen expression on her face. She looks defeated.

"Dr. Briggs, what's going on?"

Unfortunately, she doesn't have much more to fill me in on. She repeats pretty much the same thing that the nurse has told me; instead of getting a second opinion and flying that doctor here, she decided to take him to a hospital in Boston.

"Is it a good hospital at least?" I ask.

"Yes, it is. But it's the movement that's the problem. They did hire a medical helicopter, but we don't really know what kind of damage moving him in such a precarious condition will have. None of us recommended it."

I shake my head.

"Where is he?"

"Unfortunately, I can't really tell you that," Dr. Briggs says.

"What?"

"You are not technically a relative. And Mrs. Black

did not give us consent to share that information with anyone."

"I'm his fiancée! I'm the mother of his child."

"I know, Ellie. I'm so sorry," Dr. Briggs says.

"What do you want me to do? I have to see him. You're just not going to tell me?"

"Maybe you can contact Mrs. Black directly and ask her. I'm sure she won't mind telling you."

"If she didn't authorize me and took him in the middle of the night, then I'm pretty sure that she will."

"I'm sorry, Ellie, but I could lose my license over this. I really can't tell you. Medical records are confidential."

"Fuck you!" I say and storm out of the room. A dull pulsating pain runs through the hand that Blake slammed against the kitchen table. It's healing well, but anytime I get upset, the pain acts up.

"I'm going to kill her," I say, walking back and forth in front of the nurses' station. "I'm actually going to kill her."

Brie tries to calm me down. She puts her arm around me, but I just shrug her off. I'm fuming.

"Who the hell does she think she is? I mean, what gives her the right to barge in on our life and take over? Aiden hasn't spoken to her in who knows how long. He barely even mentioned her to me. And now that he's ill and completely immobile, she comes in and takes over? What the hell?"

"That really sucks, Ellie. I'm so, so sorry."

"Let's get some coffee."

I'm alert. Agitated. Far from tired. But I also feel like I need to do something and coffee seems like a good choice. We head downstairs to the cafeteria. Riding down the elevator, I'm clenching the railing so hard that my knuckles turn white. I only notice this when someone gets on and gives me a warm smile. I manage to nod back and this relaxes my body a bit.

Fuuuuuuuck! I scream inside. Why can't something go right, for once? Now, not only is Aiden in a fucking coma, but he's also somewhere where I can't find him. And the worst part? His parents don't even want me to. Well, fuck them. I'm not going to let them push me away. I love him and I'm going to fight for him. He would do that for me. I know it.

I calm down a bit when we sit down in the cafe. I sit by the window and take a few small sips of the hot coffee. I watch the steam come off the top and twirl in the light. Outside, snow is falling. A bad Nor'easter is coming. It's going to bury the whole North Atlantic coast in feet of snow. If I'm going to get to Boston, I have to go as soon as possible.

"I'm going to Boston," I say.

"What?"

"I'm going to Boston."

"But he could be at any hospital there."

"I know, but I don't know what else to do. I have to try. In reality, there are probably only a few hospitals or maybe even one that they would take him to. The one with the best doctors that specialize in this sort of thing, right?"

"I guess."

"I have to try, Brie. I don't know what else to do."

We sit for a few moments watching the snow fall.

"I'll be right back," she says after a few moments. I'm glad for the time alone. I need to figure out a plan for how to attack this situation. What would Aiden do if it were me? The problem is that Arlene has so many more resources than I do. Still, I have to try. I have to find him and I have to get her to let me see him. I can't lose him. He's my whole life.

CHAPTER 11 - ELLIE

WHEN I GO ON A SEARCH...

*W*hile Brie is away, I try to think of how I should go about finding him. The first thing I do is actually look him up online. I know that it's stupid. But he is a celebrity. Maybe someone, somewhere found out about him being taken to another hospital and posted the name of it. Unfortunately, there isn't much to be found on Google except some information about the shooting and the fact that I had killed Blake after he attacked me. Things I already know all too well.

Then I search for hospitals and doctors specializing in coma patients. Little did I know, but Boston is a mecca of brain medicine and hospitals in general. It seems like if you are afflicted with something, it's

Boston where you want to be. Frankly, I don't even know where to start. The best course of action is to go back upstairs. Someone up there has to know something. Maybe one of the nurses, or an orderly. Someone must've heard something when they were moving him. Dr. Briggs and all the other doctors have made it quite obvious that they were against the idea.

What the hell is taking her so long? I wonder.

Where are you? I text Brie. No answer. I finish my cup of coffee and head upstairs.

I walk straight to the nurses' station and find one that I remember chatting with earlier. Unfortunately, all of their names are a blur.

"I'm sorry, I can't remember your name. This has been a difficult few days," I say to the younger one. The one with the friendliest face.

"I'm Amber."

"Hi, Amber. I'm Ellie. My boyfriend, Aiden Black—"

"Yes, I know," she cuts me off.

"He was shot. They put him into a medically induced coma," I continue.

"Yes, I was here for that."

"Please, Amber, you have to help me. I went home last night and his mother just took him away. She transferred him to some other hospital, in Boston. But I don't know where he is."

"I'm sorry," she mumbles.

"Amber, I'm begging you. He's my fiancée. We're getting married. I'm carrying his baby. I need to be with him. I have to know if he's okay."

"Can't you just contact his mother?"

"That's the thing...I don't know how. She never told me she was going to do this. She just took off."

"I don't know what I can do."

I can't tell if I'm making any progress, but I continue.

"I'm sure that if you just looked through the computer, you would find his files. There must be some information here about where they transferred him to."

"I'm not sure if we're supposed to do that." She shrugs. "Private medical information, you know."

"Yes, I know. But I'm family. I'm the closest person to him and they took him away. He hasn't talked to his mother in a long time. I've never even met her and we were going to get married."

I pause. No, that doesn't sound right.

"We *are* going to get married," I correct myself. "I just want to be with him. I want to make sure he's okay."

Amber looks around. The other nurses are busy talking to each other and on the phone. One is looking through paperwork. C'mon, please, Amber, I say silently to myself. Please, help me.

"I really need your help," I whisper, leaning over the counter.

"Okay," she finally agrees. I let out a sigh of relief. Okay, okay, this is going to work.

"What's his full name again?"

I give it to her. She types it into the computer, which is facing away from me.

"Is he *the* Aiden Black?"

"Yep."

"The founder of Owl."

"Yep."

"Oh, wow, you're lucky," she says in a girly way, but then catches herself. "I'm sorry, I didn't mean it like that."

"It's totally okay," I mumble.

"Okay, let's see here. It seems like they are taking him to —"

"Amber," a low disapproving voice interrupts her.

"Where? Where did they take him?" I whisper.

"Amber, please come with me."

"Why?" she asks.

"You know quite well that we cannot release medical information to non-family members," the older nurse with big hair and an even bigger bosom says.

"Amber, where did they take him?" I plead. "Just tell me and I'll go."

Amber is about to open her mouth. But then the nurse says, "If you tell her, then you are fired."

Amber takes a step back.

"What? You can't do that."

"Yes, I can. You will be fired for disclosing private medical information to a stranger."

"I'm not a fucking stranger."

"I would like you to leave, Ms. Rhodes. I'm calling security to escort you out."

I shake my head. No, no, no. This can't be happening. I was so close to finding out.

"Please, ma'am, I don't think you understand."

"I do understand," she says calmly. The tone of her voice is ice-cold. "I'm sorry, but we cannot tell you."

I look over at Amber. Her eyes are wide and filled with horror.

I'm sorry, she mouths.

"Now, are you going to leave, Ms. Rhodes? Or shall I call security?"

"I'm going," I whisper. "I'm going."

———

I WALK DOWN THE HALLWAY. My shoulders are sagging with the weight of the whole world on them. What am I going to do now? My mind goes in circles over all the possibilities, but I come up with nothing. Turning at the corner, I disappear out of sight. I hope that's enough for now for security not to be called on me. I still have to find Brie.

"Pssst, over here." I hear Brie whisper. I turn around and see her peeking out of an office.

"What are you doing?" I whisper back. She motions for me to come over and disappears inside.

I glance down the hallway in both directions. When I'm certain that I'm alone, I duck into a little room. It's cramped and filled to the brim with paperwork.

"What is this place?" I ask, looking around a space that is only a little bit bigger than a broom closet.

"It's Dr. Briggs's office."

"What?"

"She left her laptop on." Brie sits down at the table and moves the mouse around the screen. "She's his primary doctor. There has to be something here about where they took him."

With my heart racing, I stand over her shoulder as she searches Dr. Briggs's computer. My hands get clammy and I shift my weight from one side to another to try to calm myself down.

"We're going to get caught," I whisper.

"We're not, if you keep your mouth shut. Or better yet, go act like a lookout."

I glance back. Okay, yes, I can do that.

My decision couldn't have come at a better time. As soon as I walk out of the office and close the door slightly behind me, leaving it a bit ajar, I see Dr. Briggs walking down the hall.

"Dr. Briggs, hey." I walk up to her, pulling her attention away until her back is to the office.

"Hello, Ellie," she says quietly. I'm probably one of the last people she wants to see right now.

"I'm sorry to bother you again," I say. "But is there

anything you could do? I have to find Aiden. There are so many hospitals in Boston. Can you at least tell me if he's in Massachusetts General?"

She inhales and exhales deeply.

"Did Mrs. Black tell you anything?" she asks. I shake my head. "I don't have her number so I have no way of getting in touch with her."

She takes out her phone. "If I tell you, you cannot ever say that it came from me."

"Okay, yes, of course."

"Where are you going to say you got this information?"

"I don't know," I say, trying to think of a plausible excuse. "I'll avoid it for as long as possible and then if pressed I'll say that I called all the hospitals in the area and someone finally told me. Aiden is quite famous."

Dr. Briggs doesn't seem completely convinced, but after a moment, she reads off the information on her phone.

"Dr. Shannon Duhaine and Dr. Lawrence Chapman

are overseeing his condition. Yes, he is at Mass General."

I let out a big sigh of relief.

"Thank you! Thank you so much!" I say, giving her a big hug. She pushes me away quickly.

"I didn't tell you anything, remember?"

"Oh, yes, of course."

"And he made it there okay? The move?"

"Yes, it seems like he did. It was still not a good idea."

"Yes, I agree."

"Well, I have to go. I have patients to see. Good luck with his mother."

Suddenly, I remember that Brie is still looking through her computer. I'm about to run up to her and distract her again, but luckily she walks down the other hallway and disappears around the corner.

"Brie, let's go," I whisper. "She told me where he is."

"Really?" She looks shocked. "Good. 'Cause I got nothing from her computer. It must be somewhere on the main system."

CHAPTER 12 - AIDEN

WHEN DARKNESS DESCENDS…

*T*here's no more me. I've dissipated, vanished. There's now a we. What are we going to do? How are we going to feel better? What steps are we going to take? I hear bits and pieces of their conversation. They don't think I can hear them, but I can. Crystal clear. They fight and yell and laugh. They comment on my looks. Lackluster hair. Dry face. Tired. No, that's just the fluorescent lights. HE doesn't actually look like this. Of course, he does. My parents aren't the only ones piping in. There are also the nurses. They laugh and snicker around me. They know I'm famous. The ones that don't are quickly told that I am. Others show them pictures of me in my better days. Out on the town, dancing the night away with one socialite or another. The ones that came around last night have read Ellie's books. They talk about how we met. The auction. One thinks it's romantic, another thinks it's creepy. Both of them lift up my pajama pants to take a look at my package. I don't see them, but I hear them. I can't move. I can't stop them. I want to push them away. I want to tell them that I'm here. That I matter. But I can't. I'm trapped in my body. Awake deep inside myself, but not on the surface. For all intents and purposes, I'm gone. Will I ever come back again?

I can't stay in the moment for very long. My thoughts drift away on their own accord. Ellie. They always come back to Ellie. Her soft skin. Her luscious lips. Her curvy body. Her ample breasts. Her beautiful legs. Delicate ankles. Confident hands. Soft, soft hair. And those long eyelashes. The ones that have given me butterfly kisses on my cheek. How is Ellie? I haven't heard her voice in some time now. How long, I don't know. Is she here? Will she come? I need her now more than ever. I need to know that she's here. I want her to tell me that everything is going to be okay. We're going to be together again.

Ellie's pregnant. The idea just pops into my head. It's impossible to kick back out. My girl is having my baby. What will this baby be like? Will it be a girl or a boy? Will it like trucks or dolls? I don't really care. If she's a girl who likes trucks or he's a boy who likes dolls, that's okay with me. All I want is for my baby to be happy.

Come back to me, Ellie. Wherever you are, please come back to me. I need you, honey. I need you here, holding my hand. I don't think I can do this without you. Find me. Find me. I'll be yours forever.

CHAPTER 13 - ELLIE

WHEN WE HEAD TO BOSTON…

*B*rie helps me pack for our trip. I don't know how long we will be going for so I need to bring at least a week's worth of stuff. I feel sick again from walking around for so long, so I lie down on the couch to calm down while she continues to pack.

"Are you sure you want to come with me?" I ask. "You really don't have to."

"Eh, what else am I doing, right?"

"I know, but I just feel like my life is dominating yours right now."

"You're going through a lot, El. I want to be here for

you. But if you don't want me to, I totally understand."

"Oh, no, that's not what I mean. Not at all," I say. I hate to admit it, but I need her help. I get dizzy and queasy all the time and I'm not sure I can make it there without her.

"I just want you to know that I really appreciate everything that you're doing for me," I add.

Looking through the Hotels app, I book a hotel within walking distance to the hospital. Nothing fancy, very practical, and it still comes up to over $250 a night. Oh, well, I guess that's Boston for you.

An hour later, we are finally ready to go. Brie pulls the car around to pick me up. We debated whether we should drive or fly, eventually settling on driving in case we need a car there to get around. It's only three hours and forty-five minutes away.

After making four stops, so that I could throw up and take a rest from riding in the car, we finally arrive there, five hours later. Flurries are already starting to fall and the city is bracing itself for a big storm.

The streets are empty. The few people that I do spot are half-jogging home, pulling their coats closed. Brie parks the car. We leave our bags in the parking lot. I head to the fifth floor where Dr. Duhaine and Dr. Chapman's offices are. At the nurses' station, I ask about him. They give me a blank stare, and then say they have to make a call first. Shit. After all of this, they aren't going to let me get in, are they? I wait patiently. I don't want to make a scene.

"Ellie?" A familiar voice sends shivers up my spine. I know that it's Arlene without even turning around.

"Hi, Arlene," I say.

"What are you doing here?"

"I'm here to see Aiden."

She nods and crosses her arms. I'm debating whether or not I should call her on what she did. But before I can stop myself, I say, "Why did you transfer Aiden here?"

Keep your mouth shut, I say to myself. You don't want to make this worse. You want to see Aiden, don't you?

"Why didn't you tell me where you were taking him?" I say instead.

"It was a spur of the moment decision. And I didn't even know your phone number."

"Okay," I say. That's a lie, obviously, but whatever. I'm going to let it go.

"How is he doing?" I ask.

"He's fine. He has good care here. Plus, my apartment is not too far from here."

Of course, as if that's the only thing that matters.

"Can I see him?"

She looks down at the floor and then at me. Finally, she exhales and says, "Why not."

I follow her to the last room at the end of the hallway. I run over to him as soon as I open the door. He looks about the same as he did before. Pale. Tired. Alone. But just as beautiful as always.

"I'm here, sweetie," I whisper. "I'm here and I'm not going anywhere."

I give his hand a squeeze. His fingers move a little,

pressing into my palm. My heart skips a beat. I focus on his fingers.

"Please, move again. Oh, Aiden, please," I whisper. But he doesn't move again. That must've been one of those involuntary movements they told me about.

"Visiting hours are almost over," Arlene says in the doorway.

"I'm his fiancée. I will be spending the night," I say. The tone of my voice means business. Serious. Determined. After everything that she has done, she's not kicking me out now.

Much to my surprise, Arlene doesn't argue.

"I'll see you tomorrow then," she says and closes the door.

"Oh, wow," I smile, kissing the top of Aiden's hand. "Really? Did your mom really just leave? I can't believe it!"

I lean over and press my lips to his. They are dry. Chapped. I take out some lip gloss and moisturize them for him. When they catch the light, they are back to being the beautiful luscious lips that I fell in love with.

Where are you? Brie texts me.

I text her with directions to the room and return my attention to Aiden. It feels odd to just sit here and stare at him, so I decide that the only way to make this feel normal is to just talk to him just like I would if he could hear me.

CHAPTER 14 - AIDEN

*S*he's here. She's here and holding my hand. Kissing me on the lips! Oh my God, what are you doing to me, honey? Wake me up. Bring me back to life.

"Okay, Aiden. I have a bone to pick with you," Ellie says. "Thanks a lot for *not* introducing me to your mother."

I hope you're being sarcastic, Ellie, I say. She can't hear me. I can't reach her. But that doesn't mean that I can't talk to her just as she is talking to me.

"Meeting your mom under these circumstances was not the most pleasant thing in the world, let me tell you. On the other hand, I'm not sure if it would've been much better if I had met her earlier. She's just sort of unpleasant, you know? No offense."

Oh, none taken. My mom's got her issues. She's a little high strung and she likes things the way she likes them.

"And what is up with her and your dad?"

Did they fight in front of you? They've fought plenty out here.

"They're divorced, right? I mean, what's with all of that tension if they are already divorced?"

I have no idea. I have the feeling that if someone could answer that question, they'll have the answers to all the questions in the universe.

"I don't mean to just complain about your parents though," Ellie says. "It's just that your mom had you transferred here without even telling me."

As I lay here, with my eyes closed, Ellie tells me everything that happened over the last few days. She tells me about how she met my mother, my father. About the tension between them. About my mom taking it upon herself to transfer me to another city against the doctors' advice. Finally, she tells me what she had to do to find me. How close she got and how disappointed she was when it didn't work out.

"I really thought that I may not be able to find you," she whispers. "But that's just...unthinkable."

"I missed you very much, Aiden."

I've missed you, too, I say silently.

"I just want you to know that I'm not going anywhere. I'm going to be here for as long as you are here. I'm going to wait for you to wake up however long it takes."

I love you, Ellie. I'm here. Even if you can't hear me. I know you know that I'm here. Please wait for me. I'm going to come back to you. Soon.

———

I'M NOT REALLY HERE, of course. I am and I'm not. The doctors keep telling Ellie and my parents that I'm not really here. I can't hear them. I can't see them. I can't feel them. Technically, my body is alive. My brain is functioning. The beeping EEG machine is monitoring my brain waves and making sure that it's in a certain pattern. Patients with brain injuries who are in a coma all have similar patterns. If the pattern is there, then they are comfortable that I am in a drug-induced coma. The point of this is to protect my brain.

"But what does his brain need protecting from?" Ellie asks.

"After a brain injury, the metabolism of the brain has been significantly altered," someone, presumably a doctor, says. "There may be areas that do not have adequate blood flow. The point of the coma is to reduce the amount of energy that those parts of the brain need. This will allow the brain to heal and the swelling to go down."

I'm not supposed to know any of this. I don't really hear it. But I know it. I feel it. I'm here. Not exactly alive the way that Ellie is, but alive nevertheless. Stay with me, Ellie. Stay with me until I get through this.

CHAPTER 15 - ELLIE

*T*he doctors are going to take him out of the coma. I sit by his side, watching the snow flurries fall outside the window. Everything turns white and gray, without a speck of light. I think back to our time in the Caribbean and how everything there was bursting with all of the colors of the rainbow. Bright pinks. Deep yellows. The turquoise waters that seemed like they came from another world altogether.

"We're going to go back there, honey," I whisper. "I've been thinking. And that's where I want to get married. I want to walk along the soft white sand barefoot. I want to drink brightly colored drinks with little umbrellas in them. I want to dance with you under a million stars. You just have to get better and we will go back there. You'll see."

I look at his face. Expressionless as if he were made of glass. I wait for him to squeeze my hand, but nothing happens. He hasn't had what the doctors called an involuntary response for a few days now.

"Come back to me," I say. "Come back."

Brie and the nurses come in a few minutes later. They are going to take him to another room where they will do the procedure. They've talked to all of us about this already. They need to do the procedure and they need to be prepared in case something goes wrong.

"How often does something go wrong?" I ask.

"Occasionally."

What a non-answer. I resist the temptation to roll my eyes.

"These are the best doctors," Arlene reassures me. "If they can't do it, then no one can."

I nod as if I agree. Personally, I don't see a significant improvement. At least, Dr. Briggs and her team checked in on me every day. Came in with updates. These doctors barely make an appearance. Still, Arlene is certain that they are better just because she found them. I don't have much of a position to argue from, so I avoid the discussion altogether.

Brie and I wait outside with Arlene and Dean during the procedure. Arlene and Dean sit in adjacent chairs, looking nervous. I don't know why this is a surprise to me. They've only acted in their own self-interest this whole time, hardly paying any attention to Aiden at all. And now, looking over at them, I feel sorry for them. There's a heaviness on their shoulders. If they aren't praying, they are hoping. Just as I'm about to reach out to them and say something, the nurse calls us inside.

"Everything went well. He should be waking up now," she says. I spring to my feet and burst through the door. I don't know what I'm expecting to see, but I just see him lying there.

"He's still...asleep," I say, taking his hand. "Aiden?"

"It may take him a few minutes. Or some time. It's different for every patient."

"And then...he will be okay?" Arlene asks.

"We will have to see how much of his brain function will come back."

My heartbeat skips around frantically as we wait. My hand shakes holding his, but I don't dare let go.

"Come back, Aiden. Come back," I whisper over and over.

Come back! I yell inside my head. Please come back!

Time moves like molasses. Seconds become minutes and then I lose track altogether. I don't know how long this is supposed to take, but I just wait, staring at his blank face.

"Please, please, please," Arlene says, taking his other hand and pulling him out of my fingers.

"Please, don't shake him," I say.

"I'm not!"

"Yes, you are," I insist. Our agitation and anxiety over the situation is finally spilling out and onto each other. Intellectually, I know that this is going on, but emotionally I cannot stop it.

"Ellie, look," Brie whispers. I look over. Aiden is slowly opening his eyes. Oh my God. The whole world stops all of a sudden. No one says a word. His eyelids open cautiously and then squint at the bright lights. He licks his lips.

"Aiden? Aiden?" I ask. Arlene pulls on his other arm, trying to move his face toward hers. I want to push her away, but I try to compose myself. This moment is about him.

"Come back to me, Aiden," I whisper.

———

"ELLIE," he says a few moments later. He's looking right at me. "You're here."

"Yes, yes, of course, I'm here."

"I love you," he whispers.

"I love you, too." Tears stream down my face. I can't stop any of them even if I wanted to.

CHAPTER 16 - AIDEN

I feel her there before I open my eyes. I smell her hair. I inhale her sweetness. There's a distinct smell of lavender in the air. Yet, we are not outside. Past Ellie's wide-set eyes and perfectly shaped lips, there's nothing but white. An oppressive color of white, which dominates rather than comforts.

She lifts up my hand and kisses me. I feel the tingling sensation spread through my whole body.

"Ellie," I say. My voice is rough and tired. It cracks in part as I repeat her name over and over. I don't expect her to respond. I've said her name a thousand times before to no avail. Except this time, she looks up at me with tears in her eyes. They start rolling down her cheeks as she presses my hands tightly in her palms.

"Oh my God, you can hear me," I say. Not only that, but I can also hear myself.

"Of course, I can."

I lean back in my bed and take a look around. Quickly, everything in the room comes into focus. The television on the wall. The whiteboard with some doctors' scribbles. The curtain for privacy even though it's a private room. My dad standing awkwardly at the foot of the hospital bed. The monitors next to me, beeping incessantly. My mother staring at me from the other side of the room. Is that a smile on her face? I dart my eyes back to Ellie.

"How do you feel?"

"I'm...okay."

"Really?"

"Yeah, I feel fine. What's going on?"

Ellie tells me. I've been in a coma. Eight days. It was

medically induced after I suffered a bad blow to the head. By Blake. Who else.

"Do you remember what happened with Blake?" Ellie asks.

"Yes, he cornered me on the street. But I just remember talking to him. Nothing else."

"You don't remember him attacking you. The fight?" My mom pipes in.

"No, I don't."

Two doctors come in to see me. The fact that I remember what I do is a big surprise, especially to them. They warn me that I still need to take things easy even if I feel like I'm okay.

"It sort of feels like I've been taking things easy for way too long already," I mumble. "But okay."

The doctors instruct everyone to leave to give me some time to rest. Everyone except Ellie. My dad seems to be relieved by this, but Mom is visibly upset. Still, it's doctors' orders and there isn't much she can do about it.

"I'll see you first thing tomorrow morning," she says.

"Well, maybe not first thing," I say.

After Ellie bids her sister goodbye, we are all alone. I look out of the window. Twilight has fallen and flurries are gathering.

"There's a big storm coming," Ellie says.

"Can you turn down the lights a bit?"

She dims the lights and sits in the chair next to me. Suddenly, the room is bathed in candlelight.

"I love you, Ellie."

"I love you, too."

"Thank you for being here. Not just now, but throughout this whole time."

"You knew that I was here?"

"Yeah. I don't know how, but I just felt you, I guess. Your presence. Some of the times, I actually heard you talk to me. And I talked back."

She nods. More tears come. She chokes up wiping them.

"Will you do me a favor?" I ask. She nods. "Will you climb into bed with me?"

"Are you sure? I don't want to hurt you."

"You could never hurt me."

She moves the blankets out of the way somewhat and then sits up on the bed. I run my hand up and down her back. She lets out a big sigh of relief. I push my hand up her shirt, much to her surprise. She flips her head around, her eyes wide open.

"What are you doing?"

"Touching you."

"I know that," she says with a smile.

"I missed the touch of your skin. I had forgotten how soft it was."

She gives out a moan as I run my fingers up and down her back. Her shoulder blades move up and down with each breath and she tilts her head back. I reach out with my other hand and pull on it.

"Hmmm," she moans. I bury my fingers in her hair and tug again. I want to hear her moan again. I take my hand further up her back and tug at her bra. The clasp opens up and her breasts are released.

"Oh my God, what are you doing?" she asks,

blushing. "You just woke up. Is this seriously what's on your mind?"

"I nearly died. What else could possibly be on my mind?"

She shakes her head, rolling her eyes. "I don't know if we can do anything like that."

"Oh, c'mon. Please."

"I'm serious. What if it's bad for you to get aroused, given what medication you're on?"

"I don't care."

"I do."

"Okay, okay. How about this? What if you just lay here next to me and let me touch you. Nothing else?"

CHAPTER 17 - ELLIE

I don't know why I give into him. He should be resting. He should be taking it easy. And yet, I can't stop him. I want him. I want to feel his hands all over me. I need him to touch me. I need to feel like my Aiden is back.

He runs his fingers up and down my back, unclasping my bra. My breasts fall down, freed from their enclosure. I laugh and roll my eyes, but don't protest too much. He pulls me back into his bed. I lie on top of him as he runs his fingers up and down my arms. Shivers rush down my spine. A smile forms on my face. I close my eyes and let him touch me. His fingers quickly make their way to my collarbone and then down it. My breasts move up and down with each quickening breath. He wraps my nipple in between his fingers and squeezes lightly. The space between my legs starts to feel warm. I inhale deeply and choke on my breath.

"Are you okay?" he whispers in my ear, running his tongue along my neck.

"Yes, I just got a little overwhelmed."

He slides his hand down and under my waistband. My yoga pants stretch to accommodate him. Quickly, he moves past my panties and further down. My hips start to sway without much control.

"Aiden..." I moan.

He squeezes my left nipple hard in between his fingers. It borders on pain and I let out a little yelp.

"Aiden..." I moan again. This time he squeezes it harder.

"What's my name?" he says sternly. The resoluteness of his voice makes me wet.

I turn my head to look at him. Suddenly, the sad, pale face of helpless Aiden is all but gone. There is fire in his eyes. His cheeks are flushed and he looks as determined and in charge as ever.

"Mr. Black."

"That's right. Don't forget it."

He pushes his hand further down my pants. I spread my legs to either side of the bed to accommodate him. His fingers touch the outside of my thighs and then quickly make their way further inside. But then they stop.

"Take off your pants," he instructs.

"But what if—" I start to say.

"You know better than to say no."

Just this statement alone makes me drip. I do as he says. I slide out of my pants and take my underwear off along with them. Even though the room is cold and stark, I feel like my whole body is on fire.

"Open your legs," he says. I lean back against him and open my legs, pressing my toes on opposite sides of the bed. Mr. Black pulls my body up a little further, up to his, and puts my hands on my breasts. He massages them. Softly at first, but then harder and harder. Within a moment, my nipples could cut glass.

His fingers make their way down my body. Toward my belly button, then further south. I clench my butt as I wait for him to come back inside.

"Relax," he instructs and I do as he says.

"I've missed this, Mr. Black," I moan.

"Mr. Black has missed you," he says, burying his fingers inside of me and then pulling them out again and licking each and every one. I'm too aroused to be embarrassed. He runs his index finger over my clit, pressing on it. I open my legs wider and wider, welcoming him inside.

Pushing me slightly to the side, he grabs onto my butt cheeks. He draws little concentric circles on each one of my butt cheeks as he gets closer and closer to his aim. And then he's inside.

"Sorry I don't have a proper butt plug," he says. "But my finger will have to do for now."

I swallow hard and relax my body, allowing him to get further inside.

"You're so tight. I love it."

"Mmm," I moan.

"Tell me how this feels," he instructs.

"This feels so good, Mr. Black."

"Tell me more."

"I love having you in my ass. Every movement is sending shivers up and down my body."

"Good."

"I never knew how good this could feel. It's like you're tearing me apart from the inside out. In a good way...Mr. Black."

Every time I call him Mr. Black, I feel myself getting closer to an orgasm.

"Now, open your legs up again," he instructs.

I open one so he can push his other hand inside of me. He presses hard on my clit while at the same time going deeper into my ass. I'm so aroused that even my thighs are wet. Keeping his fingers up my ass and massaging my clit with others, he suddenly thrusts three more fingers up deep inside of me. I open wider to welcome him inside and start to slide up and down. A wave of warmth starts to build up in the pit of my stomach.

"I'm going to come," I whisper.

"Not yet. And don't you dare not call me Mr. Black when you do."

This makes me even more aroused. I become completely overwhelmed. I feel like I'm going to come right this moment, but I try to hold off.

"You are going to come when I tell you to come. Do you understand?"

"Yes, sir."

"Good." He continues to go deeper and deeper inside of me. Just as I'm about to scream, he pulls his hand away, replacing those fingers on my clit with other ones.

"Come for me, Ellie," Mr. Black instructs and thrusts his fingers into my mouth. Every opening in my body is filled and I finally feel complete. As soon as I close my lips around his wet fingers, my body explodes in the most intense orgasm of my life. It comes in waves. He moves his fingers deeper and deeper inside of me. Faster and faster. I beg him to slow down, but he doesn't, pushing me to even higher heights of ecstasy. I feel the aftershocks for minutes to come.

———

"THAT WAS AMAZING," I mumble.

"I'm glad," he whispers, licking his fingers clean. "I love you, Ellie."

"I love you, too," I whisper, snuggling up to him. I'm flying on cloud nine. Nothing else matters except this moment and it doesn't seem like anything ever will again.

"Thank you for letting me do that," he says. "I needed that."

"You needed that? I needed that."

"I just felt so helpless lying here. I wanted to know if I could still be a man, to please you like a man should."

"You pleased me like a god."

"Oh, c'mon."

"No, I'm serious. That was the most intense orgasm that I've ever felt."

"I'm glad," he says proudly. "That makes me feel good."

"But how are you?" I ask. "How did getting aroused make you feel?"

"Good. Really good actually. I don't think I can have sex just yet, I'm still too weak. Even this was a little much for me, but I'm glad that I have something to look forward to."

"Of course," I say, wrapping the sheet around me tighter. Was it always this cold in this room? The sweat that I'd generated had all but dried and now turned my body into an icicle.

"I really thought I might never see you again," I say. "I mean, there was a real possibility that you would never come out of this coma."

"I'm so sorry," he says, wiping my tears. "I knew you were here all along. I just wish I could've said something. To let you know that I was okay."

"I wish you could, too," I whisper.

I lie on top of him listening to his heartbeat without saying a word for some time. He runs his fingers lovingly through my hair and smells my hair.

"Everything's going to be okay now," he says. "The worst is over."

"You're right."

CHAPTER 18 - ELLIE

WHEN NIGHT BECOMES MORNING…

I lie next to him well into the night. The temperature drops even more. I put my clothes back on and snuggle up to Aiden who dozes off. I watch the way his chest rises up and down with each breath. The color in his face is back, but his lips are still a bit dry.

"You know I can feel you watching me," he says without opening his eyes.

"Oh, I'm sorry."

"Are you ever going to go to sleep?" he asks, this time opening his eyes.

"I don't know," I mumble and rub up against him even more.

"What's wrong? You're not tired?"

"Yes, of course, I'm tired."

"Then what?"

I think about it for a moment. I mean, what is wrong? I should be ecstatic. Content. The love of my life is back and he just gave me one of the best orgasms of my life. Why the hell can I not sleep?

"I guess, I'm afraid. I really don't want this to be a dream."

"It's not a dream." Aiden shifts his body, giving me a little more room. He then pushes my hair back out of my face and runs his finger down my neck and up to my lips.

"I'm afraid that I'm going to go to sleep and wake up and not have you again. Just like before. I'm afraid of losing you."

"How about this? What if you go to sleep and I stay up? That way I'll be up when you wake up."

I consider this for a moment but then shake my

head no.

"What?" He laughs. "What's wrong with that idea?"

"That's ridiculous. You just came out of a coma. You need your rest. We shouldn't have even done what we did, let alone this. No, you cannot stay up."

"Okay, how about this?" Aiden licks his lips as he looks deep into my eyes. "We both go to sleep but only after you answer one question."

"Okay…" I say, hesitating.

"Ellie Rhodes. I love you. I've loved you since the first time I laid my eyes on you. That's why I bought you at that auction."

"I love you, too," I whisper.

"Ellie, I came to a realization today. I realize now that I want to do bad things to you forever."

I smile.

"I want to marry you, Ellie. And I want to marry you as soon as possible."

I sit up a little and look at him. We've of course talked about this before. We had plans. They fell through. We made new plans. But they were never this...rushed.

"What do you mean?" I ask.

"Just what I said. I want to marry you, but not just at some hypothetical time in the future. I want to marry you right now."

"No wedding?" I ask.

"I don't know. Do you want a wedding?"

"I've never thought of not having one, if I were to get married."

"I don't know. I guess we can talk about it. The thing that I wanted to tell you, or rather ask you is, will you marry me? Will you marry me soon?"

I think about that for a moment.

"It's not that I'm in a rush, Ellie. It's just that I came sort of close to death. And waking up now, and looking at you and being with you...it just made me realize how much I want to start living my life. I can't wait for you to be my wife and the mother of my child. I can't wait to start my life with you. Will you marry me, Ellie?"

"Yes, yes, I will!" The words escape my lips before I get the chance to stop them. But I'm glad for that. There has already been way too much thinking about this and not enough action. I love Aiden. I'm going to have his baby. Why not marry him? Why not become his wife?

I press my lips onto his and the world begins to spin.

———

THAT NIGHT I sleep like a baby. It's well into the morning when we finally wake up. And not on our own accord, but by Brie knocking on the door. When I check the time, I'm shocked to see that it's well past ten a.m.

"The nurses decided to let you sleep and get some rest since all of your monitors were showing that you are feeling good," Brie announces. She is carrying a case of three coffees and a bag of croissants. Chocolate. My favorite. I climb out of bed and grab one, handing Aiden another one.

"You look great," Brie remarks. "How are you feeling?"

"Much better. I actually got a lot of sleep last night. Didn't think I would need it since I did nothing but sleep for a week straight, but I guess I did."

Much to my surprise, the coffee and the croissant actually go down well given my tendency for morning sickness. I pop a pill to keep the nausea away and squeeze Brie's hand.

"Brie, I have something to tell you," I say, my voice shrieking in anticipation. "We're getting married."

"You are? Congratulations."

"We're getting married *soon,*" I add.

"How soon?"

"Well, that's what we want your help with. We'd like to get married very soon. As soon as possible."

"But how?"

"I was thinking maybe you could try to find a justice of the peace and ask them to come here," Aiden explains. "I'll pay however much it costs."

"You want to get married in a hospital?" Brie asks, taken aback.

"Well, no," I say. "We don't necessarily want to get married in a hospital. We just want to get married. And we're not sure how long Aiden has to stay here."

"But don't you want to have a nice wedding? Wear a dress? Invite Mom and Dad?"

"I don't know," I mumble. "I guess that sounds nice except for the Mom and Dad part."

The last bit was meant as a joke, but it doesn't come off that way.

"Brie, we're in love. We just survived this scary thing. Aiden and I could've both died. But we didn't. So, now we want to celebrate. We want to become husband and wife. Do you understand?"

She nods and looks away. Clearly, something is not registering. I don't understand why she can't be excited for me. I mean, fake it at least, if you can't be genuinely into the idea.

"Ellie, can I talk to you outside about this?" Brie asks.

I shake my head no.

"Why not?"

"Because you're going to try to talk me out of this and I don't have to listen to that. I want to marry Aiden and we're going to get married whether you help us or not."

Just at that moment, Arlene and Dean walk through the door. Out of the corner of my eye, I see the annoyed expression that forms on Aiden's face.

"Get married?" Arlene gasps. "What are you talking about?"

"Mom, I asked Ellie to marry me," Aiden says.

"Oh my God, oh my God."

"It's really not a big deal. I mean, it is for us. But it doesn't have to be for you," he says.

"How can you say that? My only son is getting married and it's not supposed to be a big deal for me? Are you kidding me?" Arlene asks.

"Ellie, can I talk to you?" Brie asks, nudging me out into the hall.

"I'll be right back." I finally give in.

CHAPTER 19 - AIDEN

WHEN SHE TRIES TO CONTROL ME...

*M*y mom isn't the most convincing person in the world but she is one of the most persistent. But her persistence isn't straightforward or direct. Instead, she will take any direction necessary to get what she wants or thinks she needs. I've dealt with these aspects of my mother for many years now and for many years I have successfully evaded her control by simply nodding along and then doing what I want.

When she starts complaining about my decision to get married, she attacks the decision first. You were just near death. You just came out of a coma. Why do you need to get married at all? Is it just because Ellie's pregnant? It's all the same bullshit questions

and statements that I've heard a million times
before, meaning my first wife. The thing to know
about my mom is that she needs to be the number
one woman in my life. She finds other women to be
a threat and will do anything to create conflict and
establish dominance. The only problem with this
approach is that it pushes me away. The last time I
spoke to my mother prior to seeing her in the
hospital happened over a fight we had about my ex-
wife. I wanted her to butt out of my marriage and
she wouldn't do it. So, I stopped returning her calls
and shut her out of my life.

And now, she's standing in my hospital room with
the air of a cruise director. She's acting as if she's in
charge. We've never talked about what happened
between us back then, and if it were up to her, she
would never talk about it again. She would be happy
just starting all over and running my life again. The
only problem is that I'm not a kid. I haven't been one
for a long time. And I've learned to stand up to her. I
glance over at my dad. He's sitting in the corner
pretending to read a magazine. The smell of alcohol
is fresh on his breath - it's either a leftover from last
night or something from this morning. Unlike me,
my dad never learned to stand up to my mother.

Even now, after their divorce, he still lets her run his life as if it doesn't belong to him.

"Mother," I interrupt her in the middle of her ongoing speech. "I am in love with Ellie. She is having my baby. I want her to be my wife."

"But—" she starts to say.

"This conversation is over."

CHAPTER 20 - ELLIE

WHEN BRIE TAKES ME OUTSIDE…

I dread going out into the hallway to talk to Brie, but I also don't want to stay behind with Aiden and his parents. I've had enough of Arlene in the days leading up to today and I'm relieved that Aiden is finally awake so that I can have some backup in dealing with her. To say that she's overwhelming would be an understatement. Now, Brie's another story.

"Brie, please don't try to dissuade me from doing this. I love him. I'm having his baby—"

"What about his family?" Brie interrupts me. I wasn't expecting this approach and she catches me off guard.

"What?"

"His family. Do you really want his family to be your family?"

I think about that for a moment. No, definitely not. I'm not sure anyone wants Arlene and Dean to be part of their family, let alone if they come as a set (which they do).

"I don't have a choice of who his family is. But we're going to make our own family."

"I know that. But…they're crazy. And what if they're around all the time?" Brie asks breathlessly. "Do you know what Arlene told me last night when we left? She said that she broke up his first marriage and that's what she'll do to you if you become his wife."

"No." I shake my head.

"Yes. Ask him."

"Listen, I don't know what happened with his first wife, but I know how Aiden and I are. We love each other. Nothing is going to happen. No one is going to break us up."

Brie crosses her hands across her chest.

"We're going to have a baby, Brie. I'm sure she's happy about becoming a grandmother."

Brie shrugs and looks at the floor. "I really have no idea. I don't think so. She's got this possessive, obsession thing with him. And Dean. But that's a whole other thing."

"Listen, I don't know what's going on with Arlene or Dean or both of them. I don't know what she did or didn't do to Aiden and his first wife. All I know is that we love each other. And we are going to get married. Now, will you help me?"

Reluctantly, Brie nods her head yes.

"And will you be happy for us?" I ask.

"Of course, I'm happy for you. I love you. And Aiden seems like a great guy."

"Okay, then please find us a justice of the peace."

———

LATER THAT AFTERNOON, we are getting ready to get married. The justice of the peace has been found. She will perform the service at three. I wait with

Aiden in his room, thinking about what I should wear. More and more snow is falling outside and the winter storm is now in full swing. Going out to get a dress or something nice to wear is completely out of the question. Aiden doesn't seem to mind. I didn't either but now I'm not so sure. Even though the elopement sounds romantic, the reality of it is starting to rear its ugly head.

I go and look at myself in the mirror. My hair is oily and stringy. I run a brush through it, but it's still crumpled and lifeless. My face is pale and splotchy. My lips are dry and lifeless. I put on some eyeliner, shadow, and foundation, but it hardly masks the problem. Suddenly, I get sick again and bury my face in the toilet. When I come back up for air, my skin is crawling with goose bumps.

Oh, how I'd give anything to feel a little bit like a bride right now. I walk back to Aiden, tying my hair up in a bun.

"Are you okay?" he asks.

I shrug. "Just got sick again."

"Are you okay to do this?"

I look into his hopeful eyes. I want to marry him. I do. But I also want to take a shower before I marry him. I want to look beautiful. I don't have to look drop dead gorgeous, but I'd like to wear at least a dress. Still, I don't really want to put this off. Aiden and I should be together.

"Do you think maybe we can have another wedding afterward?" I ask.

"What do you mean?"

"Like more of a proper one? Nothing fancy. Just…I'd like to wear something I didn't just throw up in."

He stares at me. His expression is blank.

"I'd like to have my hair done. My nails painted. Just you know…feel a bit like a woman."

I sit down on the edge of his bed, hugging my knee. I run my hand over my leg and suddenly realize that I haven't shaved my legs in days. The hard blunt hairs are coming through my pants. Perfect. Nothing makes you feel more like a woman than being a total mess on your wedding day.

"Ellie, if you don't want to do this," Aiden starts to say.

"Ellie, you don't?" Arlene bursts in. Was she just standing outside the door listening this whole time? "Of course not. I mean, you've been sleeping in this hospital room. You haven't showered. Who would want to marry feeling like this?"

Now, I hate her even more. I hate her because she's right.

"No, I didn't say that."

"Oh, c'mon, Ellie. You've probably dreamed of this day since you were a little girl. Was this how you imagined it?"

She's trying to talk me out of it. This is just a tactic. Don't fall for it. But she's not wrong.

"I did not dream of it as a little girl," I mumble. "And I want to marry you more than anything, Aiden."

I look into his eyes. This part is true. I'm not lying. I just also want this day to be special. I want to feel special.

"I want to marry you, too," he says.

"I just need some time to get ready. I'm going to take

a shower and do my hair and wear something pretty."

"Do you want me to tell the justice of the peace to wait?"

"Yes, if you don't mind. I just need an hour."

———

Yes, this is a compromise. A perfect compromise. Since Aiden is still not fully back on his feet, I grab Brie and head to the shower a few doors down from his suite. I walk inside, close the curtain, and let the warm water run down my body. Now, this is heaven. I lather my hair and wash my face. Then I shave every bit of me. By the time it's time for conditioner, I feel clean and refreshed.

"Brie, I need you to do something for me," I say.

"Can you go down to the gift shop and find me a dress?"

"They're not going to have a dress there."

"They might. And if not a dress, then something...dressy."

"I don't even know what that means."

"Just take your phone and send me photos of whatever they have there. And I'll let you know what I think, okay? Please do this for me. I don't have much time and I need to get ready."

"Fine," she says.

After getting out of the shower, I dry off and look at myself in the mirror. My face is wet, but clean and I feel like a completely different person.

"Much better," I say, wrapping my hair in a towel. "See, there's no need to postpone the wedding. All I needed was a nice warm shower."

I put on my old clothes and turn my attention to my face. Luckily, I brought my makeup bag with me and this time I'm going to go about this properly. I start with a layer of foundation and follow it up with some powder, adding highlights around my t-zone. Then I add some primer to my eyelids prior to putting on the eyeshadow. I line just the top of my lids with a thick line of eyeliner, winging it at the ends. Looking through my bag, I find both regular and water-proof mascara. I opt for the latter since it's my wedding and tears are not entirely out of the question. By the time I get to the blush and my lips, tears are already starting to well up somewhere in the back of my throat. Don't cry. Don't cry, I repeat to myself silently. You're going to ruin your whole look. I inhale deeply and try to think of something else to take my mind off this.

When my makeup is finally done, I look at myself in the mirror. Wow, perfect. Every bit of it, down to the eyebrow liner, actually come out flawlessly. No mistakes. No smudges. It is like this day is meant to be.

Now, it's time for my hair. Perhaps I should've done it first, but oh well. I spray my face with a generous amount of setting spray to make sure that it all stays in place when I blow dry my hair. Luckily, I didn't forget my wide brush, which makes blow-drying it straight a breeze. Ten minutes later, I'm almost ready. I run my fingers through my lustrous hair, wondering how it is that the shine from squeaky clean hair is so remarkably different from the oily bed hair. For one final touch, I flip my hair over and toss it around, in order to add some more body to it.

Perfect. I smile at my reflection in the mirror.

CHAPTER 21 - AIDEN

WHEN I SET UP THE SURPRISE…

"*P*erfect," I say, looking out into the courtyard. My body is still weak. I feel somewhat uneasy standing on my feet. My head hurts when I turn my neck to the right too much and when the light is too strong. But one thing is definitely perfect and that's this space.

Ellie said yes to marrying me. But I know that she has her reservations. She doesn't have a dress (not that she knows about) and we don't have a venue. I think it's okay with her if we only have a few people at the wedding, but walking down the aisle in a hospital room isn't exactly her idea of a dream wedding. And yet, here she is. Doing it for me. She wants to marry me and I want to give her the surprise of a lifetime.

Ellie Rhodes will not be walking down the aisle in sweats. She will not be standing under fluorescent lights in a bleak hospital room. I am not on death's door anymore and even though to many it seems like a rush job, I have hired someone to make this day as special for her as she deserves it to be.

Ellie is in for one hell of a surprise.

Lizbeth knocks on the door and I wave her in. I haven't seen her in ages, but she was a competent assistant on my yacht. She's an expert event planner with her own business in the making. I hired her to do this for me and I can't wait for what she is about to show me.

She walks in with a big smile on her face.

"I got the dresses," she says slightly out of breath. Back on my yacht, I've never seen her flustered even once. But this is a different beast altogether. She's putting on a secret dream wedding in the middle of a blizzard that has closed down all the stores in New England.

"I got five dresses for her to choose from. Two are from New York, one is from Paris, one from LA, and one from Miami. They are all by designers that seem to fit her style from what her sister tells me. But it would've been much easier if Caroline were still around of course. She was much more of a fashionista than her sister is."

I shrug. We all wish that Caroline was still around.

"I've had a distressed wood veranda brought into the garden out back. That's where you will exchange your vows. I've set up white chairs and brought in extra pine trees to cover up the leafless trees. Everything is decorated in lights and snow flurries."

I follow her out to the garden to take a look. It's as flawless and beautiful as she has described. The pine trees are sparkling in white lights along with yellow lanterns, bringing out the beauty in each snow flurry. The white chairs set out for guests are a divided semi-circle with a long aisle down the middle. The aisle is white, with lights going down each side.

"This is beautiful," I say and give Lizbeth a warm hug. "Breathtaking. She will love it."

"Thank you," she says, slightly embarrassed. Lizbeth isn't one for sentimentality and any expression of appreciation typically makes her very uncomfortable. I know this, but I also have to convey to her how thankful I am for making this day so special for me.

"And the guest list?" I ask.

"Everyone is going to be here."

"Her parents?" "Yes, both of her parents as well. Brie arranged that."

"Great."

"The rings?"

"They're right here."

She hands me two small velvet boxes. I tuck them into my pocket.

"Your tux is hanging back in your room."

"Thank you."

"Should I take the dresses to Ellie now?" she asks.

"Yes, I guess we're ready."

CHAPTER 22 - ELLIE

There's a knock on my door. I yell for Brie to come in. I really hope she was able to find me something decent to wear. But I don't get my hopes up. This isn't a gift shop in a resort. This is a hospital. The best they will have is a sweatshirt and maybe a new pair of leggings.

"Hello, Ellie," a familiar voice says. No, it can't be. I turn around. Yes, of course.

"Lizbeth..."

"It's nice to see you again."

"What are you doing here?"

"I'm here for your wedding."

My mouth drops open.

"I've brought you some dresses to choose from."

Now I'm entirely speechless. She leads me to an empty hospital room where I see five beautiful white wedding dresses hanging around the bed.

"I wasn't sure what kind of dress you would like to wear, so I got a selection."

"But how?"

I walk to the dresses unable to believe my eyes. Are these really mine? One is long and flowing that looks like it belongs on a Greek goddess. Another is short with a long sleeves and cream colored. It reminds me of something funky women wore in the seventies. Fun, but not exactly the right style. Three are strapless and one is made of lace. I look at the long strapless gown which has a delicate V-shape cut in the middle, intricate beading and a gorgeous hourglass outline. It also comes with a long train down the back.

"This is my favorite one, too."

"I just hope it fits," I say.

Lizbeth helps me get into the dress and brings out a long mirror from the bathroom.

"Here, put on these heels first before you look."

After I buckle the straps of my satin stilettos, I glance up. Lizbeth pins a long veil to the top of my head and I get choked up.

"No, no, no! Don't cry. Your makeup is flawless."

I sniffle and try to push the tears away. Oh my God, is this really happening? Am I really going to marry Aiden?

"I'm sorry but I don't have a capelet or anything to put over your shoulders."

"Are you crazy? This dress is beautiful. I'm not covering it up with anything."

"It's about twenty degrees outside and the temperature is falling."

"Outside?"

"Yes, we've set up out there. Everyone's waiting."

I shake my head and cover my lips with my hand.

After one last glance in the mirror, I follow her down an unfamiliar hallway.

"Your wedding will be in the garden, just out back," she explains. I thought I got to know this place pretty well over the past few days, but I had no idea it had a garden.

She takes me to the double doors and lets me peek outside. My heart skips a beat. And then another and another. More tears start to well up in my eyes. But Lizbeth pinches me and tells me to knock it off.

"You look gorgeous. You don't want to ruin it by giving yourself raccoon eyes."

I smile and then crack up laughing. Brie comes out of a nearby room, dressed in a floor length black dress.

"Oh my God, Brie." I wrap my arms around her. "You look stunning."

"So do you. I love you, Ellie. Is this beautiful?"

I peek outside again. People are starting to file through another door to the right of the garden. They are taking their seats. As more snow flurries start to fall and the lights start to flicker, the garden looks like a winter wonderland straight out of a fairy tale.

"I feel like a princess," I whisper.

"Here comes your prince," Brie says. I peek outside and watch as Aiden Black walks toward the altar in a perfectly tailored tuxedo. The suit is a perfect fit, for a perfect man. He walks with the confidence of a man who had never been inside of a hospital, in a bed, and any trace of him being in a coma is all but gone. He's my Mr. Black again.

"I'm going to go take my seat," Lizbeth says. "You look gorgeous."

Music starts to play. People turn around in their seats and face the aisle. There are my parents in the front row. Aiden's parents are on the opposite side. Everyone looks happy. Bursting with anticipation. There are no more resentments, no more protestations. Are they really happy for us? I wonder.

"It's my turn now," Brie says. "You come when you're ready."

I nod and tell her I love her. I hold the door open for her and then let it go so that no one sees me.

"Okay, okay," I say to myself. "You can do this. This is everything you have ever dreamed of."

I inhale and exhale deeply to slow down my heart rate. My hands are shaking and my knuckles are turning white. And it's not just from the cold. I'm holding a white bouquet of lilies. I bring them up to my face and inhale their sweet scent. You have nothing to be nervous about, Ellie. You are walking toward Aiden. The love of your life.

"Ms. Rhodes?" an unfamiliar voice calls my name just as I'm about to open the door. I turn around and see two men dressed in police uniforms standing next to me.

"Yes?"

"Ms. Rhodes, you need to come with us," the taller one says, taking off his hat. I narrow my eyes. What is he talking about?

"Ms. Rhodes, you are under arrest. Please come with us."

I stare at them dumbfounded.

"Under arrest? For what? This is my wedding. I'm about to walk down the aisle. Can't you see that?"

"We are here to arrest you, Ms. Rhodes, for the murder of Blake Garrison. I'm sorry but you will not be getting married tonight. You are coming with us."

I shake my head and turn toward the door. I look at Aiden's strong jaw and his hopeful eyes looking down the aisle. He's waiting for me.

"I'm sorry, I can't come with you. I'm getting married," I say, still not fully grasping the situation in its entirety. When I reach for the door, one of the cops grabs my arm and pulls it behind me.

He holds onto my wrists tightly until he secures them behind my back with handcuffs and then pushes me down the hallway, away from Aiden.

"No, please, you don't understand. I'm getting married."

"No, you don't understand. You, Ellie Rhodes, have the right to remain silent. Anything you say can and will be used against you in a court of law. You have the right to an attorney. If you can't afford an attorney, one will be provided for you. Do you understand the rights I have just read to you?"

I shake my head no. No, no, no. I don't understand anything. My head starts to buzz. My legs go limp. I trip and the cops put their arms under my elbows and practically carry me out of the hospital. The cold wind hits me like a ton of bricks. Tears run down my face. What is happening? Why are they doing this to me?

CHAPTER 23 - AIDEN

I stand at the alter waiting. I wait and I wait. The temperature drops and eventually I wipe the smile off my face. Brie is standing opposite me with a perplexed look on her face.

Where is she? I mouth to her, hoping that no one else sees it. Brie shrugs and looks around.

She's supposed to come right after me, she mouths back.

Is she really not coming? Dark thoughts start to swirl around my head. No, not Ellie. She wouldn't just stand me up. She wants to marry me. Right?

I stare at Brie and she stares back at me. Finally, she looks back at Lizbeth. I follow her gaze to the back of the room. Lizbeth is nowhere to be found either. I saw her come in, but now she's gone.

I prop up my smile even though I'm starting to hear the guests starting to whisper. My mother is about to approach me, but my father has the good sense to keep her down. Finally, Lizbeth appears again. She has a crestfallen expression on her face. I hold my breath as I wait for her to walk down the aisle.

"Ellie has been arrested for murder," Lizbeth says and my world turns to black.

CHAPTER 24 - AIDEN

WHEN SNOW STARTS TO FALL...

I'm holding my breath. My heart is pounding in my chest. About to pop out. I inhale and my throat seizes up. She's about to be my wife. It's almost time. We're going to be together. Forever. Despite everything. In spite of everything. We're finally going to have our happily ever after.

Snow is starting to fall, covering the ground in pure white. Seconds melt into minutes. Time is passing like molasses and flying by at the same time. I'm about to see her. We're about to begin our lives together.

My thoughts drift back over everything that has happened since I met her. I remember the way she

looked standing on that stage on my yacht. She was
the last person in the world who would have
auctioned herself off to the highest bidder. It's just
not the type of game that she was going to play. But
I'm glad she did. As soon as I saw her standing there,
the bright spotlight blinding her, I knew that I had to
have her. I had to make her mine. And that was
before I even got to know her.

As we started to spend time together, I got to know a
whole different side of her, Ellie. Kind. Sweet.
Loving. A wonderful friend. Someone who did not
deserve any of the heartbreak that followed. It's the
darkness that pushed us apart at first, but then
brought us closer together. I was there for her.
Through what happened to Caroline. And she was
there for me. Through me losing my business, the
thing that I'd built up from the beginning and the
thing that I'd thought was my whole life, until I met
Ellie. And then she was there for me after what
happened with Blake. He tried to push us apart. He
tried to take her away from me. Agh, just thinking
about this now, makes my blood boil. He put me in a
coma, nearly taking my life. And then…then he did
something even more unforgivable. He went to take
Ellie's life. Ellie's, and our unborn child's life.

My throat clenches up with anger. I ball my fists. I shouldn't be thinking about this at a time like this. It's in the past. It's all over. I'm standing at the altar waiting for my love to walk down the aisle and begin our lives together. This is a good day. I'm going to put Blake out of my mind. Completely.

I wait and I wait. Then I wait some more. People start moving around in their seats looking around. The atmosphere in the garden is starting to lose its magic. She should be here already. Why isn't she coming? My heart sinks. Is she having second thoughts? Cold feet? What if she doesn't want to marry me at all?

No, that's not it. I know that she wants to be with me. Deep inside, beyond all the doubts, I know this much is true. I may not know much about anything anymore, but I know that Ellie loves me.

Of course she loves me. But marriage? A sudden wedding? I sprung that on her out of the blue. I was so happy to be alive again, to be breathing and talking, that I needed to grab life by the horns. The trauma had left me feeling lost. I needed to get back my confidence. My arrogance even. I wanted to be Mr. Black again. And in order to become Mr.

Black, I needed to make a statement. To make her my wife.

And now, standing here at the altar, waiting for her, I wonder if that, too, has been a mistake. In my long line of mistakes. Perhaps, I was forcing her. Pressuring her to make this commitment that she didn't really want to make. I know she loves me. She wants to be with me. But marriage? That's not necessarily something you want to jump into after a near-death experience. Or maybe she did want to jump into it at first, but then she started thinking about it all in more detail and that's when all the doubts started to creep in.

My hands are starting to freeze. I press my fingers against my sides to try to warm up. The guests are no longer hiding their concern. Some are straight out standing up and looking around. My mom, the perfect specimen of a mother (I'm being sarcastic, of course), is twirling around and whispering to whomever will listen. I can't really make out what she's saying, but by watching her lips move I can tell that she sure is saying Ellie's name a lot.

I inhale deeply and exhale even longer. How long should I stand here before giving up? I don't really know. I peer into the back of the aisle in search of a sign. What if the hold up has nothing to do with cancelled plans? What if she had some sort of wardrobe malfunction and I ruin the entrance by leaving my post too early?

No, if that was the case, someone would've come up here and told me. Right? Okay, i'm going to give it a few more minutes. That's probably as long as I can bear standing up here with all of their eyes on me. Pity. Sadness. Sympathy. That's what the guests are all saying with their downcast looks and their jittery bodies.

I glance at Brie, who gives me a brief shrug. I search the room for Lizbeth. She was just here and now she's not. Suddenly, she re-appears. No smile. Not even a wink. There's a sadness that's settled onto her porcelain face. A heaviness that's resting on her shoulders. What is it? What's wrong? I want to yell out. Her walk down the aisle takes what feels like forever. Finally, she's within earshot. She leans closer. I can see her labored breaths against the cold air. Puff. Puff. Puff. Little clouds that escape her lips and disappear before reaching mine.

"What?" I ask, not fully grasping what she says. She repeats herself.

"What?" I ask again.

"Ellie has been arrested for murder," she says again. This time, I hear her. I hear her, but I don't exactly process it.

CHAPTER 25 - AIDEN

WHEN I SURPRISE MYSELF…

hough I don't quite understand the words that have come out of Lizbeth's mouth, my body seems to. For a moment, everything turns to black. My vision gets blurry and disappears completely. It's as if I am looking through a telescope and I close my eyes. But then a moment later, I open them. At this moment, everything becomes crystal clear. My thoughts come into focus. And I know exactly what to do.

I open my mouth and start rattling instructions.

"Call Bill Whitney. He's with Whitney, Thompson, and Rodriguez."

Lizbeth nods and starts to type everything I say into

her phone. Bill doesn't sound like much of a name, but he's one of the best criminal law attorneys out there. My business lawyers are always going on about how great he is. I've met him on a few occasions, social fundraising events. But I haven't had the opportunity to see him in action yet.

By the time Lizbeth dials his number, we are back in my room at the hospital. I've given instructions to her and pretty much anyone else who would listen about cleaning up the wedding party and made brief apologies about the postponement. They are no longer my concern anymore. Only Ellie is. She's the only thing that matters right now.

"Hello, Mr. Whitney—" Lizbeth starts to say when she gets him on the phone. I take the phone away from her.

"Bill, this is Aiden Black. We met a few times back."

"Yes, of course," he says in a groggy distant voice.

"My fiancée has been arrested for a murder she did not commit. And I need your help."

The details are ironed out quickly. He says he will be here soon. He will be taking a private plane out of

New York, which I of course will pay for. In the meantime, he will be sending another attorney to meet me at the police station right now.

"Our goal is to make sure that she does not say anything incriminating to the cops, which would make all of this much harder."

"Incriminating? But she's not guilty," I say, quickly jumping to Ellie's defense.

"Yes, of course. But that doesn't mean that the police can't turn her words around and make her say something that she doesn't mean. Innocent people incriminate themselves all the time."

I arrive at the police station ready for a fight. I'm wearing a well-tailored suit. My hair is brushed. My armor is up. I'm here to rescue Ellie, if that's the last thing I do. Bill's proxy, Thurston Daniels, is already here. They say I have to wait in the lobby. I can't go in the back. I can't talk to the cops. I just have to wait and wait. And then wait some more.

When I thought that time was passing slowly at the altar, now it's positively crawling by. I read all the magazines. I drink ten cups of shitty, lukewarm, yellow coffee from a vending machine. A few people who work at the station come over to tell me how much they like using Owl. None of them are cops, but I appreciate the compliments. One of them even goes so far as to say that they were assholes for firing me in the first place.

I continue to wait. Lizbeth joins me. I ask about going to see Ellie again. Again, I'm not allowed. She tries as well, but the police officers remain unwavering. I get another big lump in the back of my throat. But my faith in Bill and in the legal system remain steadfast. She is innocent. Blake attacked her after he attacked me. He was going to kill her. She killed him in self-defense.

All of that is true. But how did they get enough evidence to arrest? The District Attorney had to sign off on this. So, what is it that they have on her that I don't know about?

CHAPTER 26 - ELLIE

WHEN I'M INSIDE...

The cell smells of urine and sweat. I'm alone here, but it's definitely big enough to hold more people. But tonight there is no one else. Is that a good thing? I don't really know. Perhaps. But it would be nice to have someone to talk to. To vent about the fact that they arrested me at my wedding. Right before I walked down the aisle. I'm still wearing my fucking wedding dress, for crying out loud!

How could they do that? Who gave them the right? They stopped me from even telling Aiden what's going on. They just snatched me up, leaving him all alone up there. What if he thought I had cold feet? What if he thinks that I don't want to marry him?

I bury my head in my hands. This isn't the time to think about any of that. Sitting here, in a fluorescent bright room, without a ray of natural light or even a sense of what time it is, the last thing I should be thinking about is how they ruined my wedding. I should be thinking about the fact that I was wrongfully arrested for killing a man who attacked me. Who tried to kill the love of my life and put him in a coma. But somehow none of that matters that much now. All that matters is Aiden. I close my eyes and take my mind back to him. To his beautiful face and his luscious lips. To the way he possesses both kindness and toughness at the same time. I have to hold onto him to get through this. I have, I need to believe that this is all a big mistake, in order to survive.

I look down at my stomach and cradle it in my hands.

"It's going to be okay, baby," I say to my unborn child. "Your daddy is going to make everything okay. I know it."

———

MY ATTORNEY, Thurston Daniels, arrives sometime later. There's no clock here and they took away my phone, so it could've been half an hour later or four hours, for all I know. He's a serious, no nonsense type of man with gray hair and dark eyes. He introduces himself and asks me if I talked to anyone about anything. I shake my head no. He asks me again, just to double check. Suddenly, I'm relieved that I didn't have anyone in the cell with me. I probably wouldn't have been able to abstain from talking to them.

"What about the cops?" he asks. "What did they ask you?"

I shrug and gloss over the details. "They asked me stuff, but I said I was waiting for my lawyer. I'm sure glad that you showed up. 'Cause that was a total lie."

I smile at him, trying to break the ice. But he's either not the type to smile or isn't in the mood. Instead, he excuses himself and disappears for a while. I'm left all alone again with nothing but dark thoughts circulating around me.

How do people spend years here? Let alone, how do

they do time in solitary confinement? Especially the innocent ones. The ones who were convicted of crimes that they didn't commit. How do they spend years sitting here in these bright, windowless rooms and wait their life away on appeals? It has barely been a few hours and I'm ready to claw my eyes out. My only consolation is my baby.

"I'm here, honey," I speak out loud. "We're going to get through this. Daddy is going to help us. We won't be here for long."

But no matter how much I talk or stare at the textured concrete walls, Thurston Daniels doesn't return. Not for a while.

Long after I get tired of waiting, I finally give up and lie down on the cot. I've fought against this. I've sat on the edge, as if that would somehow make the time pass more quickly. Lying down is some sort of defeat. It's accepting my fate of spending the night at the police station. But the pregnancy and all the ups and downs of the day - getting arrested at my own wedding and all - have sucked all the energy out of me. I lie down and close my eyes. And just like that, I'm somewhere else. I'm walking down the aisle. I'm beautiful and radiant. And since it's my imagination, we are not getting married in the hospital garden in the middle of a snow storm, no matter how nicely it's decorated. Instead, we are somewhere warm. The sun is shining and the water is so blue and clear that you can see all the little yellow and blue fish swimming around the bottom. Aiden is waiting for me.

When I walk up to him, he gently lifts up my veil and I lose myself in his eyes, which are wet with tears. He tells me he loves me and vows to always be there for me no matter what. I promise the same thing in return. The details of the vows aren't clear to me now. The only thing that is, is how much I am loved in this moment. And how that love we feel for each other will never vanish or fade. But only grow stronger.

"Ellie. Wake up. Ellie."

There's a pounding on the door. Brutish and loud. A harsh disagreeable voice yells my name. When I open my eyes, I'm back in jail. My head is pounding. Throbbing. My mouth is parched and I realize that I haven't had any water in a long time. As soon as I sit up, I feel queasy.

"You're out on bail," the same voice says, hitting something metal against the door. The sound is so shrill that it sends shivers down my body.

"You're outta here," he says, opening the door. When I walk past him, he hisses, "at least for now."

Blood drains from my extremities and my fingers turn to ice. What does he mean by that? What the hell does he have against me? Thoughts start to swirl around in my head, making me feel even more sick to my stomach. I follow him out through the double doors into the main room. That's when I see him, Aiden. My Aiden.

He's sitting on the bench at the far end of the police station with his head hanging down. His fingers buried in his hair.

"Aiden!" I say meekly. My voice breaks in the middle of his name, but he still hears me. When he looks up, our eyes meet and the defeated expression on his face vanishes immediately. He jumps up to his feet and practically teleports himself across the room.

"Ellie, oh my god, how are you? Are you okay?" He takes me into his arms. The sweet scent of vanilla takes all of my worries away. I nod and tears start to roll down my cheeks. He wipes them off and then buries my head in his shoulder.

"It's going to be okay. Everything's going to be okay."

It takes me a few moments to calm down a bit. But I finally get it together. I wipe my eyes and then rub the remnants of the wetness on my dress. Oh my God. I'm still wearing my fucking wedding dress. What a sight! A bride on her wedding day lying in a holding cell. How pathetic. And wrong.

"How are you...standing?" I ask after a moment. "Are you okay?"

Aiden smiles.

"A little tired, but okay."

"Oh my God." I wrap my arms around him. So, he's okay. Almost all okay.

"I was only using the wheelchair around the hospital as a precaution. I'm okay. Medically that is."

I know what he means.

"Take me away from here," I say, taking his hand. He

gives a squeeze and leads me outside. I don't know if everything is going to be okay for good. All I know is that it's okay for now. And that's good enough.

CHAPTER 27 - ELLIE

WHEN WE DEAL WITH LAWYERS...

*W*hat follows is largely a blur. Days pass as we meet with my lawyers, or rather the lawyers that Aiden hired for me. They devise a strategy. They make calls. They change the strategy. Finally, Bill Whitney goes to have yet another chat with the District Attorney. When he comes back, he isn't as calm as he was before.

"Why didn't you tell me?" Bill demands, furrowing his brows. Aiden and I are sitting around the hotel suite. We ordered room service. The food is still sitting under those silver domes on the delivery tray.

"What are you talking about?" I ask.

"He said that they have your journal."

"My journal?"

"You've kept an online journal. You wrote that you wanted to kill Blake."

"Oh, that."

"Yes, that," he says. The tone of his voice is scolding. Disapproving. Who does he think he is to talk to me this way? Especially, since he has no idea what he's talking about.

"It's nothing," I say with a shrug. "I was just venting."

"Well, it looks like premeditation."

"Well, it wasn't. I was angry at Blake and I was just expressing myself."

Bill paces around the room. "That's what I'm trying to convey to the DA, but so far he's not buying it."

"So, what does that mean?" Aiden asks.

"He thinks, or at least, he acts like he has a case. I'm trying to convince him that he doesn't. If I can, then he will drop the charges."

I take a bite of my salad.

"The problem is that these DAs have gotten really

big heads. With all the mandatory minimum laws it's no longer the judges who are in charge of making decisions. It's the DAs. If they decide to charge you, if they decide that they have a good enough case, then they move forward."

"But this has nothing do with a mandatory minimum."

"Yes, I know. If you are tried and convicted, you will go away for a very long, long time."

His words send shivers through my body.

"It's just that the mandatory minimum laws have given district attorneys way too much power and they are a bit drunk on it. Especially, this one."

I take a few more bites of my salad. The chewing is so loud inside of my head that it somewhat drowns out all the fears and the doubts.

"But it's going to be okay, right?" Aiden asks.

"This online journal isn't a good thing. I really wish you hadn't written those things."

"I know, I'm sorry. But honestly, I was just venting. Writing is my way of expressing myself."

Bill shakes his head.

"Yes, I know," he says, raising his eyebrows. Another sign of disapproval. What the hell is this guy's problem?

"What does that mean?" I ask.

"Well, your writing is kind of a problem. You see, you're not the most sympathetic defendant out there."

I shake my head and narrow my eyes.

"Why are you giving me that look?" Bill asks. "You don't believe me?"

"I don't really appreciate your tone, Bill," Aiden steps in. "What exactly do you mean?"

"Your girlfriend writes porn. If this goes to trial, the jurors aren't really going to understand that."

I gasp.

"I do not write porn. I write romance novels."

"A series of novels where a woman is auctioned off to the highest bidder? With extensive sex scenes? With bondage, and anal plugs?"

His words make my skin crawl.

"I'm sorry, Ellie, I know that this is the twenty-first century and all and women are out there reading and watching Fifty Shades of Grey. But there's no guarantee that regular women, normal women, who will be on your jury will understand that. Especially, when the DA reads some of your writing on the stand."

I shake my head and look away from him. Is he really saying this to me? My cheeks flush with anger.

"How dare you?" I say, feeling my blood starting to boil. "I write romance novels. Yes, they have sex scenes in them. But so what? That's what people do, you know. Have sex. There's nothing wrong with that. My characters are in love. My stories are about how no matter what happens, you can get through anything as long as you have love."

"That may be the case, but that's not what the jury is going to see. The DA will read some of your literary stylings and paint you with the brush of a sex maniac. He will say that you are not the norm. That only crazy, sex-crazed women would read the smut that you write. He will make you into a villain."

"I don't like the tone of your voice, Bill," Aiden says. "Can we tone it down a bit, please?"

"I'm just telling you the truth. But I guess that's too much for you two."

"No, what you're saying is your opinion."

"My expert opinion. After many years of legal experience."

"Bill, I hired you to represent Ellie in this case. I did not hire you to berate her and make her feel bad about what she does."

"No, the jury will do that all on their own."

I stare at him. His bald head. His pin-like eyes. His soft jaw and protruding stomach. Suddenly, it hits me. He is getting a kick out of this. He is actually getting off on putting me down.

"Do you have a problem with me?" I ask after a moment.

"No, of course not."

"Because it sounds like you do. Do you have a problem with my writing?"

"Your writing? I couldn't care less about your writing."

"So, why is it making you so mad?" I ask. I'm trying to stay calm. But below the surface, I'm fuming.

"I'm not mad. I'm just expressive."

I shake my head.

"Listen, you can do whatever you want," Bill says. "I'm just telling you what people are going to think about your so-called books."

"My so-called books?" I repeat his words back to him. Something about this man isn't right. Not at all.

"Listen, Ellie, I've read your books. Some of them. What I could get through anyway," he says, rubbing his temples. "They are not my cup of tea."

"They are not written for you," I say.

"But you think you can just write anything you want and publish it and put it out there, huh?"

CHAPTER 28 - ELLIE

WHEN THE TRUTH COMES OUT…

$\mathscr{I}$ stare at him, dumbfounded. Yes, in fact, I know that I can write something and publish it if I want to. Something's wrong here. This guy, Bill Whitney, has a problem with me and it has nothing to do with the case. No, this goes much deeper than that.

"Yes, I clearly do think I can do that," I say sternly. "What I mean is, that I write the stories that I want to write. I publish them. People seem to like them. Love them actually. I have a number of people writing me how much they enjoy my books. But what am I doing wrong again?"

"So, this, what you are doing, you think this makes you an author?"

I put my fork down and lean back in my chair. I glance over at Aiden, who seems to be just as dumbfounded by the whole situation as I am.

"Yes, that's exactly what it makes me."

"Agh, I'm sorry," he grunts, throwing his hands up in the air. "But I don't think so. Writers are vetted. They work hard on their writing. They spend hours editing and proofreading."

"And who told you that I haven't?"

"They submit their manuscripts to agents. They get dozens of rejection letters. They keep submitting until finally someone takes them on."

"Bill, I think we're getting off track here," Aiden says, trying to veer the conversation back to the case. But I put my hand on his. I want to hear this.

"Or you can do all that work and just put the book out yourself," I say. "I won't lie. I did what you are talking about as well. But no one took me on. So, one day, I said, fuck it. I'll just put my books out directly to the readers. Who knows, maybe they'll like them. And guess what? They did. And guess what? That's what EL James did, too. Sometimes, it takes a whole bunch of readers to get someone in the publishing industry to finally take an interest in your books. They can be a bit behind the times."

Bill shakes his head.

"No, I refuse to understand that."

"Well, you don't really have to," I say sarcastically. "You could just accept it, like gravity."

Perhaps, that was a bit too much of a sarcastic smartass comment, but he's really getting on my nerves now. He's supposed to be my attorney. We're not supposed to be here debating the state of the publishing industry together. I mean, what the hell does he care about it anyway? Unless...

"It just pisses me off," Bill says. "I worked and worked on my thriller. A good one, too. Nothing worse than what John Grisham writes. And no one cares. I mean, I submitted it to everyone. And then I published it myself. Crickets on both accounts. Nothing. Sold maybe a few copies to family and friends."

I can't believe the words that are coming out of his mouth. So, his problem with me is that he's angry that his book isn't selling? Yet, instead of asking me for help, for some advice about how to advertise, he just goes on a rant about my own work? What an asshole.

"I think I need a new attorney," I say, turning to Aiden. Normally, I would keep my mouth shut. Bite my tongue. But not this time. I have too much on the line and I've been through too damn much. I'm no longer the quiet, meek girl I was before. No, this time, when someone offends me on purpose, they're going to hear about it.

"What?" Bill asks with a slight gasp.

"I need a new attorney," I say loudly. The tone of my voice is definitive. Decided. My mind is made up.

"What are you talking about?" Bill asks. He is only now realizing that he has underestimated me.

"They arrested me for a crime I didn't commit. The last thing I need right now is some wannabe writer complaining about the quality of my writing just because you can't sell your book. That's not my problem. And I don't need you representing me if you feel that way about me."

Bill's mouth nearly drops open. "I didn't mean anything by it," he starts to say, but I don't want to hear it. I've listened enough.

"I can't trust you," I say. "You go off on a rant about my writing. First, you say the jury won't understand me. Won't sympathize with me. But then the truth comes out. You are just a jealous asshole who wants to put me down. Well, I don't have time to deal with your ego. I need an attorney who believes in me. He doesn't have to like my writing, but his goal should be to have them let me go free. Not to help them put me in jail."

"That's not my goal," he mumbles.

I just roll my eyes. "Sure sounds like it."

And with that, the conversation is essentially over. Bill continues to make an effort to explain himself, but just ends up digging himself into a deeper hole. He talks and talks as Aiden walks him out of the hotel room. But none of the words he says go one step in the direction of trying to explain how he's going to attempt to deal with the District Attorney. Instead, he just tries to explain himself and apologize without actually apologizing.

After Aiden closes the door, he walks over and takes me into his arms.

"You are...amazing," he whispers.

I smile and kiss him on the lips.

"That was unexpected," he continues.

"You aren't mad?"

"Mad? Why would I be mad?"

"That I fired this wonderful lawyer you found for me," I say. "I don't want you to think I'm ungrateful."

"Oh, hell no. That guy was an ass. And the sooner we got rid of him the better."

"Really?"

Aiden presses his lips to mine and, for a brief moment, I feel like it's all going to be okay.

"We're going to find someone much better tomorrow. Someone who will believe in you and have a good rapport with the DA."

"I like that," I say.

CHAPTER 29 - ELLIE

WHEN WE HAVE SEX…

I never knew what people were talking about when they said that there was a comfortable silence between them until I met Aiden. Around him, I don't feel the need to chat non-stop and fill the air around us with useless words. It feels good to just be with him.

I lie down on the bed and Aiden lies down next to me. He practically nuzzles up next to me, putting his head on my arm. I glance down and see how his biceps flex with each movement and something stirs within me.

"Hey there," I say with a wink.

Aiden narrows his eyes, assessing the situation. "Hey there," he responds.

I decide against beating around the bush. "I want you."

"Oh, really?"

"Yes, really," I say.

"Hmm, I don't really know if I'm into it right now," he says. Is he joking? I can't tell.

"Ellie," he says, turning my head toward him. "I'm not serious, you know."

A big smile comes over my face. The goofy expression on his face disappears and he leans in and brushes a soft kiss against my lips.

"I missed you," I whisper. I look up at him. There's that familiar gaze of adoration. It's more than just infatuation, something from afar. No, this is different. He's looking at me and really seeing me. For who I am.

"I want you," I whisper. He closes his eyes and then opens them again.

"You're the most beautiful woman in the world," he

says. I know with every fiber of my being that he's telling the truth.

Aiden leans close to me. He presses his lips onto mine and pushes his body onto mine. His lips are now forceful. Stronger. More powerful. I feel every muscle in his body and the strength of him is disarming. It's as if every part of him is saying that nothing bad can ever happen with this man by my side.

His kisses get harder and harder. Each one borders more and more on pain, but the good kind. The kind that sends shivers through my whole body. As I push back at him, I feel him rise above me, just a little bit, and then we melt onto the bed.

Quickly, our bodies begin to move as one. I feel his manhood in its full glory, bulging out of his pants. I take it out. I have to see it. I need to feel it. His hands make their way down my body. There is no trepidation or hesitation. He's an expert now. He knows exactly what I like.

A few quick movements and I'm suddenly completely undressed. He is shirtless and his hard chest is heaving over me. He slides his hands back up and across the curves of my hips. He kneels down and runs his tongue up around my hipbones. He veers north toward my belly button, teasing me and making me wet. Then he makes a quick turn south and heads toward my thighs.

As I lie down on my back, I see the way that my body rises and falls with each breath. I close my legs forcefully to keep myself from getting too aroused, but it's too late.

"I'm so...hot," I whisper, burying my hands in his hair.

Aiden continues to tease me. He kisses me along my non-existent panty line, well below my belly bottom, but not quite all the way in between my legs. Before he even reaches inside of me, I feel a wave of pleasure start to build in between my thighs.

"Oh, wow, you are aroused," Aiden says. Before I can confirm, he thrusts himself inside of me releasing a waterfall of emotion.

"Aiden!" I whisper breathlessly. Riding the wave, I grab onto Aiden's firm buttocks and squeeze as hard as I can. They feel firm and powerful in my hands and I use them to guide him in and out of me.

"That was fast," Aiden whispers in my ear, kissing my neck. Now he is comfortably inside of me, making himself at home. This is the way it's supposed to be, I think. This feels so right.

But as he glides in and out, slowly at first, and then faster and faster, the area in between my legs starts to beg for him. I yearn for him.

I feel his whole body tense up as his movements get faster and faster. I wait for him to climax, enjoying each moment, and then another wave of pleasure thrusts through me.

"Oh..Aiden!" I moan his name in pleasure.

CHAPTER 30 - ELLIE

LATER IN BED…

*L*ying in the afterglow of all that romance, and love, and sex all balled into one, I feel much better about my whole predicament. There's something about releasing all those endorphins that suddenly makes it feel like everything's going to be okay in the end. Besides, I'm kind of a sap. Optimist, if you will. I believe that everything is going to be okay in the end. And if it's not, then it's not the end.

I glance over at Aiden who has his head propped up with his hand. He's lying on his side with the sheet just covering him a little bit. I bite my lower lip because I sort of want him again.

"Don't take this the wrong way," he says.

"What?"

"You promise?"

I narrow my eyes and look him up and down. "Well, I can't really promise anything like that, can I? Until I know what you're going to say."

"Okay, okay." He waves his hand. A big smile broadens his face.

"What? What is it? You're freaking me out."

"Okay, don't take this the wrong way, but I'm starting to see the baby."

I glance down at my quite visible stomach. It's bigger than a pouch now. Now, there's something definitely in there.

I give him a little wink.

"You're beautiful. So, beautiful," he whispers. "I just can't believe that you're having my baby."

I shake my head and bury my face in his shoulders. It's hard to explain how it feels to have someone be there for you through your pregnancy. This would be the hardest part of my life up to this point even if

I weren't going through all that other stuff. And to not have him beside me right now and fully supporting me? Well, I just don't know. I have mad respect for all those single mothers out there and pregnant women who are doing it on their own.

"Why did you think I would get offended?" I ask after a moment.

"I just wanted to convey that I think you are beautiful. I didn't want you to think I thought you were fat or anything like that, just because you are showing so much."

I look down at my belly again.

"Am I really showing that much?"

I stand up and walk over to the floor length window. Oh. My. God. I am showing. A lot. This baby is practically protruding out of me. It's funny how days tend to pass without you really looking at yourself. I mean, I've taken showers and gotten ready. But I haven't really seen myself.

"The baby is quite big now," I say.

"How far along?"

"Um, let's see." I try to count back to the last time I saw the doctor. It wasn't that long ago. And yet, I have practically no memory of it.

"It's either nineteen or twenty weeks now," I say. "I think. The last bit of time is all blending together if you know what I mean."

"I wonder why."

I go back to the bed and sit down next to him. I wrap myself in the sheet and run my fingers through his hair.

"So, I was thinking," he says after a moment. "What do you think about finding out the gender?"

I smile. I've been meaning to talk to him about that, but there wasn't really any time.

"I really want to know," I say. "I wasn't sure if you did though."

"I do," he says.

"But my doctor is back in New York. And I'm not allowed to leave the state."

Wow, those words sound so odd coming out of my mouth. I am actually out on bail. I'm prohibited from leaving the state. Whose life is this? Definitely not this quaint little English major who spent all of her days reading books and writing stories.

"That's okay. I can schedule an appointment with someone here."

"Okay, let's do that," I say as he pulls me back on top of him. "By the way, that's not really what it's called anymore."

"What do you mean?" Aiden asks, moving a few strands of hair out of my face.

"Gender. I mean, they do call the parties 'a gender reveal,' but it's not really the gender that we're finding out. It's the sex."

"What's the difference?"

"Gender is a socially-constructed concept. People are born a particular sex and then they become a specific gender. Like someone can be born a woman with a vagina, but they may grow up and identify themselves as a man. She may feel like more of a man so she can then refer to herself as a man and use the 'he' pronoun."

Aiden thinks about this for a moment. "That makes sense."

"So, when we go get an ultrasound, we will find out the sex of the baby," I clarify further. "Do you care what it is?"

"You mean, boy or girl?"

I nod.

"Not one single bit," he says almost immediately.

"Really? I thought that guys always wanted to have a boy."

"And I thought that girls always wanted to have a girl," he challenges me.

I shrug. "You know, come to think of it, I don't really care either. I'm actually excited to find out."

CHAPTER 31 - ELLIE

THE FOLLOWING AFTERNOON...

*T*he following morning we meet with more lawyers. I'm still getting used to just the kind of important guy that Aiden is, because they all come to our suite. I thought we would spend the day waiting in big glass buildings where everyone is dressed in expensive suits, but instead he doesn't even get out of his pajamas. I get dressed up by putting on a pair of leggings.

We meet with three attorneys, each one seems sort of like the other. We talk briefly about the case and ask them questions about their other clients. Aiden really takes this part over for me. He feels terrible about what happened with Bill Whitney and his unprofessionalism and is making up for it by grilling the new prospects. When the last one leaves, he turns to me to see what I thought.

"I really don't know." I shrug. "I mean, how do you even evaluate how good a criminal law attorney is anyway? Until the thing goes to trial, that is."

"Let's hope that it won't get that far."

"Really? Is that still a possibility?"

"I have hope," Aiden says, tilting his head. "Hey, what do you think about Thurston?"

"The lawyer who got me bail? He seemed alright."

"He was very eager. But also confident. Not lazy," Aiden says, measuring him up. "I'm going to have another chat with him."

I smile at him. I like seeing him back in command. After watching him lying there lifelessly in the hospital room, this is quite a change. It reminds me of the man I first met. The man who I fell in love with. That arrogant, cocky stranger who bid on me at the auction. I get a little excited thinking about that again.

"What is it?" Aiden asks, sensing my change in mood. I smile a little at the corner of my lips.

"What?" he asks again, pulling me closer to him. I sit down on his lap. I lower my head and kiss him on the lips. He reciprocates by pressing into me. I run my fingers over his hard chest. He buries his head in my hair, sending shivers down my spine.

"Are you in the mood for a little break?" he asks.

"Depends. What do you have in mind?"

"I want to do bad things to you."

"Oh, really?" I feel myself get a little flushed.

"Mr. Black wants to do bad things to you," he clarifies. I close my eyes. I've been wanting to do something like this for some time now.

"I'd like that," I say slowly.

"You'd like what?" Mr. Black asks.

"I'd like for you to do bad things to me…Mr. Black." My whole body tenses in eager anticipation of what's to come. I point my toes to release some of the tension, but it's to no avail.

"Hmmm, let me see," Mr. Black says. He raises his chin, lost in thought. "How shall I punish you, my dear?"

There's that word again. Punish. It's unassuming and not at all dangerous and yet it makes my heart jump into my throat. In a good way.

Without another word, he suddenly opens his legs and pushes me onto my stomach on his lap. He's careful to make his way around my belly, making more room than necessary in between his legs. With one swift motion, he pulls down my pants, exposing my butt.

Suddenly, my whole body starts to shake. In a good way. From anticipation. We've never done anything like this before and the excitement is even making me sweaty. Mr. Black runs his hand around one of my butt cheeks, giving me a little smack. Then he does the same thing to my other butt cheek. Moving the rest of me closer to the ground, so that my head is practically resting on the floor, he opens my legs.

"Wider," he instructs and I do as he says.

He takes his finger and pushes it inside of me. I

exhale deeply. He takes his finger out of me and licks it.

"Delicious," he says. I feel myself blush. I move my head to look at him, but he pushes me back down.

"I didn't say you could look."

"Can I?"

"No," he says, slapping my butt. "And you are supposed to call me Mr. Black, remember?"

I nod.

He grabs my butt cheeks with both hands and pulls them apart. I moan in pleasure. Then he runs his finger around my butt and inner thighs, toying with me. Large concentric circles become smaller concentric circles. He focuses his energy around my core, but he doesn't dare touch. Games. Games. Oh, how I love his games.

A moment later, he is inside of me. In my ass. He pushes his finger deeper and deeper and I moan louder and louder. With his other hand, he presses on my clitoris and begins to rub.

"Oh....Mr. Black," I moan. Just calling him that gets

me wet. But just as things get even more exciting, he stops.

"Noooo," I complain. But he just rearranges me before him. He takes his tie and ties my hands behind my back. Then he opens his fly, pulls down his pants, and positions my face in front of his hard cock. Then he opens my mouth and slides inside. I suck and lick until my jaw feels like it's about to clench shut. He moans my name and it sends shivers down my spine.

Just as he is getting close, he pulls out.

"Oh, please?" I moan. "Will you come for me, Mr. Black?"

"No," he says categorically. "You are going to come for me. When and where I say."

My body thrusts into a cold sweat. I'm both excited and scared at the same time.

He pulls me up to my feet. Keeping my hands tied behind me, he flicks one of my nipples and then the other with his finger. Then he puts one in his mouth as he massages my other breast. The space between my legs starts to throb. I step from one foot to another trying to calm myself down. Mr. Black grabs another tie and ties it around my eyes. Now, I can't see anything.

"Sit down as if you were sitting on a chair," he instructs. I do as he says. "Now, open your legs. Wide."

Again, I do as he says. "Wider."

Now, I'm balancing on the balls of my feet, with my womanhood opened wide in front of him. I can't see a thing, but suddenly, I start to feel everything. Every breath he exhales. Every tense muscle in his body.

He presses something cool and hard against my clitoris and begins to move it up and down. I'm so wet that it glides along easily, adding to the sensation. He walks around me, keeping his one hand on me and then pushes something smooth and hard inside of my butt. It's small, but it fills up every space within me.

"Oh my..." I whisper.

"Yes?" he asks. I can sense the smile on his face.

"Oh, Mr. Black," I say. The sensation is

overwhelming me. At any moment, I'm about to burst.

But right before I do, Mr. Black stops.

"Get on your knees," he says. I do as he says. He unties my hands and ties them again in the front. Then he pulls me forward.

"Follow me," he says. I follow him on my knees across the room. Occasionally, he stops and I suck on him until he tells me to stop. He ties my hands to something hard. He doesn't let me get up. Instead, he pulls my butt up higher in the air.

"Now, we're really going to have some fun," he says. With that, he pushes the familiar smooth object inside my butt as I moan from pleasure. Then he pushes something big and hard inside of me and turns it on. It starts to vibrate, sending impulses through my whole body. Another part of it presses on my clit, only intensifying the sensation.

My eyes roll to the back of my head, even though I'm blindfolded.

"Mr. Black," I moan.

"Yes?" he asks, turning the speed up and sending my moans into overdrive.

"I need to come."

"No," he says. "You will wait until I say so."

I try to hold on. I grab on to something that feels like a bedsheet in front of me and dig my fingers into it. Just as I think that I can't hold on any more, he pulls away from me.

Again, he pulls me up to my feet. This time, I can barely stand up. I'm angry with him. Furious. How dare he not let me experience pleasure? Who the hell does he think he is? What if I can't get there again?

And just as I'm about to call him an asshole to his face, he clips something cold and sharp onto my right nipple. Then my left.

"What's that?" I ask. It feels...good. There's a little weight to them and they are connected by a chain. The clips send a tingling sensation through my body, especially when he plays with them with his tongue.

"Hmmm, that feels...good," I whisper.

"I'm glad," he says sternly.

He pushes me back down on my knees.

"Follow me," he instructs again. I do as he says. My nipples burn a little as the chain moves along with me, but in a really arousing way. What's next? I wonder. I don't think I can handle much else.

Just then, my legs run into something round and hard and he guides my body up and down onto it. It's like a desk except that it's soft and cylindrical. Mr. Black unties my hands and ties them around this object. I lie down on it with my ass exposed on the other side.

Mr. Black walks all around me, running his fingers over my back and down my butt cheeks. Then he inserts the familiar hard object back in my ass. This time, I almost come as soon as he touches me with it.

"No, not yet," Mr. Black says, and I do as he says. I'm expecting him to finally glide himself inside of me. I'm practically begging him to. But he doesn't. Instead, he walks around and pulls my head up by my hair. He thrusts his large cock inside of my mouth and then pulls on a string, activating the object inside my ass.

"Oh my God," I mumble with my mouth full of him. With each thrust, he pulls on the object a little more and I squeeze my butt cheeks in pleasure.

After a few moments, I'm dripping wet. He pulls out of my mouth and finally glides inside of me. Deep. Strong. His thrusts fill me completely.

"Come for me," he says and every inch of my body fills with warmth and pleasure before he finishes his sentence.

While I'm still in full swing of my pleasure, he starts to move faster and moan louder. A few moments later, he yells my name and collapses on top of me, completely spent.

CHAPTER 32 - ELLIE

WHEN WE MAKE PLANS...

The following morning, we manage to finally untangle from one another and leave the hotel room. I had forgotten how much I have missed actually being with Aiden. It's not just the sex though. It's the way he makes me feel. Loved. Protected. Understood. Seen. Our sex life is an expression of that. I can give into him because he is there for me. I can give up control and let go because I trust him implicitly. In addition to my lover and fiancé, and soon the father of my baby, Aiden Black is also my best friend.

It's a cold dreary day where the clouds are hanging far lower than they have any right to. What is it about the cold in the Northeast that chills you down to your bones? As soon as I opened my eyes this morning, I knew that the last thing that I wanted to do is go outside today. But Aiden insists on it. He got us in to see one of the best OBGYNs in the Boston area and she is squeezing us in between patients. Basically, this is a big favor. So, we can't just not show up.

"But it's raining," I complain as I am getting dressed. "And I'm pregnant."

"So?" He laughs, putting on a nice pair of slacks and a dress shirt. No tie. Only a jacket.

"Don't I get to not do things I don't want to do when I'm pregnant?"

"Yes, typically. But not when it comes to going to the doctor. Besides, we're going to find out the sex today!"

His eyes light up at the statement. He's really excited to find out. Don't get me wrong. I am, too. But I'm also really tired and run down. Just standing up is making my head swim.

"Okay, how about this? If you hurry and go, I will get you anything you want afterward?"

"Anything?" Now my eyes light up. Aiden nods, handing me my coat.

"How about I never have to go again?" I joke, but only partly. Seriously, I hate going to doctors. And I particularly hate going to see gynecologists. That's one of the reasons I never have until I got pregnant. Doctors are a fear of mine. An irrational fear, I know. But what fears are rational? Aren't all of them irrational simply as a result of the fact that they are fears?

"How about we get some ice cream on the way home?" Aiden asks. "A gallon of whatever you want."

"It's freezing out!" I stare at him, dumbfounded. Shocked by the fact that he would even suggest such a thing.

"So? It's ice cream. It doesn't matter what time of year it is."

I follow him out of the door, shaking my head.

"You have to be kidding," I say. "I only eat ice cream in the summer."

"How could I not know that?" he asks. "I think I have to re-evaluate this whole relationship now. No, I don't think I can be with someone who only eats ice cream in the summer."

There's a town car waiting for us right outside the door, so I don't have to spend much time in the freezing cold drizzle. The town car is warm and inviting and there's even a little coffee machine in the back. Aiden makes me a little cup of tea to warm me up even more.

"God, I wish I was pregnant in the summer. I'm so cold all the time," I moan. Aiden just takes my hand and gives it a little squeeze.

We arrive at a beautiful glass medical building fifteen minutes later. The driver drops us off right in the front and Aiden holds my hand as we make our way inside. Riding up the elevator, I expect that this whole procedure is going to follow the usual process. First, I'd have to fill out about a million forms on a clipboard. Then I will have to wait as the office manager enters all that information into the computer and makes calls checking to see if I do indeed have insurance and how much co-pay they will have to charge me. All of this back and forth typically eats up an hour or so. But much to my surprise, we are cordially invited to the back room right away after I tell them who I am. No clipboard. No co-pay. Not even giving out my insurance card.

"What's going on?" I ask Aiden as the nurse shows us to the room.

"I told you they're doing us a favor." By us, of course, he means him. No one would do me this kind of a favor in a million years.

Once we're in the room, which is about double the size of the one in the last place, the nurse asks me to step on the scale. I put my purse on the chair along with my jacket and walk over to where she's waiting. My heart sinks. I don't want to weigh myself.

"Wait, I'm still wearing my shoes!"

"It's okay," she says. Except that it's not. I don't want to be weighed with my boots on. Or my heavy sweater. That's going to add like ten pounds. Ten pounds that I definitely don't need. Don't they have one of those little paper nightgowns around? As soon as the numbers are about to show up on the screen, I look away. Then I close my eyes for good measure. If there's one thing I definitely don't want to know is how much I weigh.

"Too scared to know how much you've gained?"

"I feel like I've gained a hundred."

"You are actually at a very healthy weight," she says. "But I won't tell you if you don't want to know."

"Thank you, I appreciate that."

Aiden just rolls his eyes. "I keep telling her that she looks beautiful. Drop dead gorgeous."

I blush. I love when he says stuff like that, but I'm a little embarrassed about having the nurse hear it as well.

After the nurse leaves, we are left alone for a few moments. She doesn't tell me to change so I remain sitting on the table in my normal clothes.

"This is just an ultrasound," Aiden says. "I don't think think they're going to do an exam."

"Good, I hope not."

"I know you don't like doctors, but I'm here for you. I'll be here for you through everything, okay?"

I nod. He doesn't really need to constantly reassure me, but it sure does make me feel better about everything.

CHAPTER 33 - ELLIE

WHEN WE FIND OUT...

I open my phone and start scrolling through the numerous emails that I have had piling up over the last few days. Most are from my readers. They love the series and can't wait for the next book to come out. I love how much they love my books, and I feel guilty for not working on it as much as I should be. The funny thing about writing is that though it can be so hard to get going, especially when you have a whole bunch of bullshit going on in your life, it's the exact thing you need to get you through everything. There's nothing like sitting down at the keyboard and diving head first into another world.

I take the time to write back every person who

reaches out to me over email and on Facebook. Many writers don't, but I'm grateful. And thankful. Because of my readers, I am able to do something for a living that is my dream. I am living my dream life. They allow me to do this and, for that, I will forever be grateful.

"How's everything going with your writing?" Aiden asks. We haven't talked about it for some time, so I catch him up on the details. I'm working on my last book. I want to tie everything up together nicely and give the couple a happy ending. But this is the really hard part. To make sure that they have their happily ever after, and this ending is actually authentic. I've read plenty of books where people ended up together, but their union seemed forced. Almost for no other reason except that this is what is expected of them.

"I'm sure you will do a good job," he says.

"Thanks." I nod. I love how supportive he is of me, despite the fact that this career of mine might have caused him trouble in his own career.

"So, you don't mind me writing this?" I ask after a while. "I mean, I was thinking about what Bill said."

"Don't give that asshole a second thought."

"Yes, I know, I know. I won't. The thing is that I was just thinking about the fact that what I've written is so close to life. I wonder how much of an impact it had on your shareholders and everything that happened with Owl back then."

"What you write is fiction, Ellie."

"Yes, that's what I say, of course. I mean, the names are changed. There are parts that are heavily elaborated. But between you and me, it's not entirely fiction. As you know. You did buy me at an auction."

"The thing is, the way I see it, this is the twenty-first century. Women have the right to do whatever they wish and that includes expressing themselves sexually. Your writing is just that. An expression. So, whatever may or may not have happened as a result of that, it's really their problem. Not ours. You are a wonderful writer and you deserve to do what you do. And there are people out there that love what you write."

I take his hand in mine and give it a strong squeeze. He doesn't really get it, and he probably never will, despite how many times I tell him, but it means the world to me how much he supports what I do. I didn't grow up in a family that had much respect for writers - I mean, they enjoyed literature and reading, but they didn't exactly think that it's the right career choice for anyone, let alone, their daughter, to pursue. And now that we're starting our own family, it's amazing to have someone by my side who not only supports me but also celebrates me. There's nothing like it in the world.

There's a knock at the door. A woman who is only a bit older than I am walks in. After introducing herself and shaking our hands, she asks, "Okay, are you ready to find out the sex of the baby?"

My heart skips a beat and then another. Aiden squeezes my hand in anticipation. I lie down on the table and pull up my shirt. Dr. Dillard puts some gel on my stomach and places a wand on it. We all look at the monitor next to me. I see the little head on the screen. Lots of squiggly lines. Everything in black and white. As she presses down on my lower stomach, I feel the baby move. The feeling is surreal. Some women fall in love with their babies in utero. But that hasn't happened to me. I've never really planned on having kids. I've barely given it any thought at all. And yet, here I am. Lying here with

Aiden by my side, looking at our baby, I feel surreal. How is it that I have made a baby? And it's actually going to come live with us? I know this sounds almost ridiculous. But for someone who never planned on having kids, the idea of having a baby is more than just a bit surprising.

"So, do you want to know the sex?" Dr. Dillard asks. Aiden and I exchange looks.

"Yes," we say simultaneously.

"Good," she says, moving the wand around. "I'm glad that you're both on the same page about this."

Aiden and I look at her with anticipation.

"You're having a boy," she says.

I look over at Aiden. A boy. Oh my God. I'm having a boy.

"Oh, wow," I mumble.

Dr. Dillard tells us more things, but frankly it all goes in one ear and out of the other. I can barely understand a thing that she's saying. My focus is entirely on the sonogram. I'm having a baby boy. I'm having a baby boy. Oh my God.

I glance over at Aiden again. He can't really contain his excitement either. Prior to leaving, Dr. Dillard says that he looks like a very healthy baby. When we're finally alone, Aiden throws his arms around me and gives me a warm hug.

"I'm stunned," he whispers in my ear.

"Me, too."

CHAPTER 34 - ELLIE

WHEN WE FIND OUT...

*I*t takes a bit to settle into the idea of the fact that we're having a baby boy. To say that I'm feeling excited would be the understatement of a lifetime. On the way home, Aiden and I stop into a Whole Foods and pick up five quarts of ice cream. We debated whether we should get one large gallon, but couldn't decide on the flavors. So, we finally split the difference and just got five different types. Rocky Road. Chocolate. Raspberry Dark Chocolate. Coffee. And strawberry vanilla swirl.

Though the day wasn't particularly stressful or eventful, by the time we get home, I'm fully drained of energy. These days I seem to have very little energy altogether. Usually, I wake up tired and if I do anything at all, then my energy resources are depleted. Going to the doctor today and getting the news has left me completely exhausted.

"All I want to do is take a hot shower and then eat the entire quart of rocky road ice cream," I say, walking to the elevator of the hotel.

"Oh, but I thought that you didn't eat ice cream when it's cold out?" Aiden jokes.

I roll my eyes at him. "That's why I'm going to take a hot shower first. So, I'm warm before I have something so cold."

Though it's early afternoon, I have the whole day planned out. Nothing but my pajamas, Netflix, and ice cream. If I feel sick to my stomach, I may have a salad. Maybe.

Unfortunately, life has other plans. As soon as we get back to the suite, Thurston shows up, the attorney who got me out on bail. He's acting like my main counsel until we figure everything out a little more.

"So, what's going on?" Aiden asks.

"Well, I talked to the DA. Things are a bit up in the air," he says in his monotone voice. There is no expression on his face so I have no idea if that's a good thing or a bad thing.

Probably sensing my confusion, he explains further.

"Things could be better," he says. "They have your online journal where you say that you want to kill Blake. That's what is making the DA's office think that maybe this wasn't self-defense."

"But it was—" I start to say. He cuts me off.

"I know. I think the best thing we can do is to have a little sit-down with him. He knows that you have representation. And typically the best thing to do is to not talk to the DA. But I really want to prevent this from going to trial, if at all possible."

"Is that possible?" Aiden asks.

Thurston nods. "I think so. Ellie...is as close to a perfect client as you can get. You are law abiding, you went to an Ivy League school. You pay your taxes. Yes, you write fiction, sometimes it's a bit erotic. But this is America. Nothing illegal about that."

"So, you don't think the jury would take it the wrong way? Would think I'm a terrible person because of that?" I ask.

"I don't know what the jury would think. My goal is to prevent that from happening," Thurston says. "That's why I want you to meet with the DA. I need him to see you as a full person. I really cannot let this go to trial."

"Just curious," I say. "What if it does?"

"Well, it's not good. The problem with trials is that they are completely unpredictable. You just never know when you're going to have that one jury member who decides to sway the rest in one direction, or holds out on everyone. And the thing is that district attorneys rarely take things to trial unless they are certain of a guilty verdict. So, it's my job to do everything in my power to prevent that from happening."

My throat clenches up from fear. A million what-if questions start to ruminate around my head. What if the DA cannot be swayed? What if he hates me the way Bill Whitney did, for no reason whatsoever?

What if this does go to trial? What if they convict me?

Sensing my turmoil, Thurston puts his hand on mine. "Please don't worry. Everything is going to be okay. I'm going to schedule a sit-down with the DA and we're going to get all of this worked out."

CHAPTER 35 - ELLIE

WHEN WE BREAK THE RULES...

I shouldn't go see her. I am not allowed to leave the state of Massachusetts. But the problem is that I am not so sure if I will ever leave this state. Nothing is figured out yet with the lawyers. We're still waiting to see when I can get a meeting with the Assistant District Attorney and the main detective in charge. Thurston is trying to shield me from the truth, but I know that if they decide to take this to trial, who the hell knows what will happen. Thurston is trying to stay positive. Everything is going to be okay, he keeps saying. But I'm not so sure. And the closer it gets to the meeting, and possibly the trial, the worse it will be to go.

It's not going to take long. Just a short trip there and

back. It's only to Connecticut. But I don't have a car.
And I can't really rent one in my name if I don't
want anyone to find out about it. Yes, I mean
anyone.

I don't want Aiden to know. I don't know what his
reaction will be. But as that saying goes, it's better to
ask forgiveness than to ask permission. I have a
feeling that he will not want me to go. I have a
feeling that he will try to dissuade me. Convince me
to stay. Tell me that I can go see her later. But neither
of us know if this is actually the case. What if the
meeting doesn't go well? What if they take the case
to trial? What if I'm convicted? Then I will never be
able to stand by her gravesite and talk to her
ever again.

Aiden has meetings all day. He is going to New York
and then coming back late this evening. This is my
opportunity.

"Are you sure you're going to be okay here?" he asks.

"Yes, of course. I've got a bunch of shows lined up on
Netflix and the fridge is full. My day is all set," I lie. I
feel a little bad about lying, but I'm just trying to
protect him.

"Order some room service if you want a real meal," he instructs.

"I will. I will," I say. "Okay, go. Don't you have to be at the airport soon?"

"You realize that it's my plane, right?" he says, putting on his coat. "They'll wait for me because I'm the only one going on it."

"But don't you have to be there by eleven for your meeting with the shareholders?" I ask.

"Yes, I do." He hangs his head. "But maybe I can just postpone it? Don't you need me here?"

He's looking for an excuse to stay, but I can't give him one. Instead, I give him a brief kiss on the cheek and shuffle him out the door.

As soon as I'm alone, I check my phone. Once again, I debate the pros and cons of renting a car. It would be much faster, of course, but the problem is that I have to give my name and credit card. There would be proof that would be too easy for someone to find. Now, if I take a bus or a train, then it would be much harder to spot me. I use cash to pay for my ticket and, though they could find me on the surveillance footage at the terminal, there will be tons of people there so it's pretty unlikely. The train ride is about $200, but it's three hours shorter than the bus would be. So, train it is. The next train leaves in half an hour. If I hurry, I can make it.

————

I FIND a seat in the back of the train car, next to the window. I would love to spend the day lying around in bed watching Netflix and doing absolutely nothing useful, but this is the only day that Aiden is going away. The last thing I want is for him to get involved with this. I'm breaking the rules of my bail and, if I get caught…No, I can't even think like that. Getting caught means that I would have to spend the rest of the time waiting for trial in jail. My heart sinks. What the hell am I doing? If you get caught then you'll lose everything.

For a second, I debate whether I should just get off at the next stop. Maybe this is stupid. But then my thoughts drift back to Caroline. She may not be here anymore, but that doesn't mean that I can't go see her. I've never visited anyone at a gravesite before, but I just know that I will feel her presence at hers. I close my eyes and drift off.

The next thing I know, I'm in Greenwich. I hail a cab and give him the address of the cemetery. Then I ask him to wait at the entrance with the meter running. He seems only too happy to do that.

I remember exactly where she is buried and I head there directly. It's starting to drizzle and I regret not bringing an umbrella.

"How could you come here without an umbrella?" I hear Caroline ask.

"How was I supposed to know it was going to rain?" I ask out loud.

"Um, you could've checked the weather. Duh," she says.

"Hey, listen, I'm not the type to always carry an umbrella. Mainly, because I know that I won't melt into the ground if I get a little wet."

No matter where she went, no matter the time of year, Caroline always carried a little umbrella in her purse. Her hair was of absolute importance. She absolutely hated getting wet and refused to buy one of those little cheap umbrellas that vendors sold on the streets once it started to rain.

Finally, I get to her grave. It's a simple gravestone with her name, Caroline Elizabeth Kennedy Spruce, and her birthdate. Underneath it says, Beloved Daughter.

She was so much more than just a daughter. I'm sure that her parents loved her and she loved them, but they were not very close. And yet, in death, that is all she seems to be. I guess you can't put 'best friend and a girl who loved nothing more than to have a good time' on a slab of rock.

CHAPTER 36 - ELLIE

I stare at the gravesite, watching raindrops collide with it. What I would give for an umbrella right now, so I could shield her headstone.

"Hi, Caroline," I say quietly. "I know what you would say right now. What the hell am I doing here in the middle of a rainstorm? Well, you see it's either now or never. I don't really know what's going to happen with my arrest. I might be going away for a long time. A very long time."

Just saying those words out loud sends shivers through my body. I shudder and wrap my hands stronger around my shoulders.

"The thing is that I wanted to come here and tell you something," I continue. "You were my best friend. No, you are my best friend. There's no one else like you. So, as soon as I heard, I knew that I had to tell you."

I take a deep breath.

"Caroline, I'm having a baby. A little boy."

The words hang in the air above us as I choke up over my tears.

"I know you weren't much into kids, at least that's what you always said. And that's what I said as well. But it's really different now that I'm the one who is pregnant. And I know deep in my heart that if you were here right now, you would feel different about kids, too, knowing that your best friend was having one."

I take a deep breath and wipe some of the tears. But more quickly take their place.

"I want you to be the godmother of my baby. I know that you are not particularly religious and neither am I. But to me, having a godmother means that there's always someone out there that loves my child as much as I do. And I want you to be his godmother...even if you are not around anymore."

My nose is running along with my eyes and it's all mixing with the raindrops thundering on me from the sky.

"Will you be his godmother, Caroline?" I ask. I wait for her to respond even though I know that it's stupid and futile. And then, much to my surprise, a loud roar of thunder rolls in.

Yes, yes, the thunder says. And the sun peeks out slightly from behind the far away clouds.

"Thank you," I whisper. "Now I know that my baby boy has someone to watch over him. You will be there for him no matter what."

Another roar of thunder rolls through.

I wipe my tears and kneel down next to the headstone. I put my hand over her name.

Why did you leave me that note, Caroline? I ask, only this time, I don't say it out loud. Why did you want me to know that it wasn't an accidental overdose? Was that supposed to make me feel better about this whole thing? Like, it's something you wanted? Well, I know you, Caroline. I know that this was not something you wanted. This was the last thing you wanted. That decision, it was just a spur of the moment thing. Something stupid. You didn't really mean it. Did you?

And then it hits me.

"You wanted me to know how badly he had hurt you," I say. "Didn't you?"

A bolt of lightning flashes through the sky.

"You wanted me to know that it wasn't an accident," I say and another bolt strikes through the clouds above my head.

"The DA will be pressing charges against Tom," I say. "He reached out to me. He will be pressing charges against him for what he did to you and I will testify on your behalf. I will tell them what happened that night, if it's the last thing I do. I will testify even I have to do it from jail."

Another bolt of lightning strikes and I bury my head in my hands and crouch further down, almost entirely onto the wet soggy ground. My shoes and the bottom of my pants sink further into the mud.

I don't say anything else after that and I do not hear any more thunder or see any more lightning. As I walk back to the cab, I wonder if I am just a silly girl who talked to herself at that cemetery and all that ruckus that I heard was nothing but weather. Perhaps. Probably. At least that's what my head says. But deep within my heart, I know the truth.

When I get to the cab, I tell the driver to take me back to the train station.

"Do you have a family member there?" he asks. I shrug and nod.

"Yep," I say. It's not a lie at all. Caroline is like family to me.

"I'm sorry about that. Did they die young?"

"Yes, very young. She was my age."

"That's horrible," the cab driver says. We sit in silence for a while. There's something about the topic of death that makes it impossible to take the conversation further. If I don't explain who died and why, it's too uncomfortable for the other person to continue pressing the issue.

The rain clears up a bit on the short drive back. I

look at my phone. A missed text from Aiden. He's going to be back at the hotel a bit later than he thought. Good. That gives me a bit more time to get back.

A loud screeching of tires breaks my concentration. A strong forward momentum slams me into the plexiglass separation between the front seat and the back seat. Everything turns to black.

CHAPTER 37 - ELLIE

WHEN I REALIZE WHAT HAPPENED...

When I open my eyes, I find myself in a daze. There are red blinking lights everywhere around me. People are gathering and staring into the back seat. Someone opens my door and helps me out. My first thought is no, no, no. I shouldn't be here. And all of these people should not know that I'm here.

"Are you okay, miss?" someone asks me. When I look up, I see that it's the cab driver. I've only seen him from behind the wheel, so it's kind of a surprise to see him in front of me. He is much taller than he seemed before.

"Miss, are you okay?" he asks again. I just realize that I haven't responded to anyone for a while.

"Yes, I think so," I manage. He takes his hand and helps me up to my feet. I look around. The back of the car in front of us is all smashed in.

"What happened?" I ask.

"He got into my lane without using a turn signal and then stopped short!" my cab driver starts to rant. I immediately regret the fact that I even asked.

The other driver responds with a completely different story and they start to bicker. Okay, Ellie. Think. You are still in Connecticut. You need to get to your train. It's a long ride back.

"Well, the cops will be here soon." I hear my cab driver say. My heart sinks. The cops! No. I can't have the cops taking down my name or anything else.

"Listen, I have to go. I have a train to catch," I say.

"No, you can't go."

"Yes, I can. The train station isn't far from here."

"I need you as an alibi. You have to give your testimony."

That's the last thing I intend to do.

"I didn't see anything," I say. "Honest. I was looking through my phone and just felt the impact."

"Well, you don't have to say that," he says with a wink.

"Oh, no, no, no. You are not going to coerce her into lying," the other driver butts in and they start to yell at each other again. I use this opportunity to quietly walk away from the scene. I walk across two lanes of traffic and take the next exit off the highway.

Unfortunately, I am still quite far away from the train station. It didn't look that far on my phone, but then I realize that was the driving time. It's definitely too far to walk.

Okay, what to do. I look around the quiet suburban street. Nothing but SUVs and two-car garages everywhere. This isn't New York. There's no way that I'm going to be hailing a cab around here any time soon. And this is not exactly the type of neighborhood where there's a bus stop anywhere nearby. No, my only option for getting to the train station on time is to get a ride share. Uber or Lyft. I turn on my phone and click on the app. I know that it's possible for them to track me here, but I'm not really sure if it makes sense to keep all of this a secret anymore. Still, it's best if I'm the one who comes forward with this. The last thing I need is to get caught across state lines without a particularly good explanation.

The rest of the trip is pretty uneventful. I manage to take the train that's only half an hour later than the one I planned to take and I will be back at the hotel way ahead of Aiden. Grabbing a seat by the window, I start to obsess about my options. One option is that I don't tell anyone about my visit. No one has to know, right? Well, that would've been the way to go before the accident. I bought my train ticket with cash. I took a cab. Again, paying in cash. All of these things ensured very little possibility of tracking. But now that I was in an accident, everything is different. I had to take a ride share to get to the train station. That means there's a record of me paying for an Uber using my phone in Connecticut. The app doesn't accept cash and everyone's names are visible and recorded. Of course, just because this information exists, it doesn't mean that the DA in Boston or in New York has to find out about it. But it does mean that I won't have a good explanation for any of it if by some crazy chance they do.

My thoughts go back and forth about all the possible eventualities. I am still completely undecided when I walk through the doors of the hotel and head up to our suite. Okay, stop thinking about this, I say to myself to calm myself down. You have plenty of time to decide one way or another. No one knows yet. Just get back, start the bath, and dig into a bowl of ice cream. That will clear my head real fast. But as soon as I open the door, my mind goes blank.

"Hey, where were you?"

Aiden is sitting on the couch watching a game on TV. He's dressed in sweats. He has been here for some time. How long, I don't really know. When I thought that my mind was running in circles before, it doesn't even compare to what's going on now.

Just when I am about to answer, Thurston comes out of the guest bathroom.

"Oh, good, you're here," he says. "I was able to get us a sit-down with the assistant DA and the main detective about your case for tomorrow."

Tomorrow. The word just hangs there in the air, as if it's suspended on a string.

I stare at them both dumbfounded. I don't know what to say.

"What's wrong?" Aiden asks. "You look like you've seen a ghost."

Something like it, I think to myself.

"Thurston wants to go over your story," Aiden says. "I guess story is the wrong word. He wants to go over what happened. Why don't you grab some food and have a seat."

He points to the room service cart in the middle of the room. I walk over to it slowly.

"Aren't you going to take off your coat?" Aiden asks, furrowing his brows. Yes, of course. I look down. I'm still wearing my boots, scarf, and jacket.

"Oh, wow, your shoes are so dirty," he adds. "What happened?"

CHAPTER 38 - ELLIE

WHEN I GET CAUGHT...

I walk back to the foyer trying to think of what to say. What possible explanation I could have for all of this. But nothing comes to mind. I undress slowly, trying to buy some time. Then I head to the bathroom inside the master bedroom.

"Hey, are you okay?" Aiden knocks after a few minutes. I'm hiding out. I don't know what else to do.

"Yes, I'm fine," I say. "I thought that you were going to be in New York."

"We got finished early."

Just my luck, I mumble.

"Ellie, what's going on?" he asks. I shrug as if he can see me. I don't respond. He knocks again.

"I'm just not feeling very good," I finally say.

How long can I seriously keep this up? Thurston has set up a meeting with them for tomorrow. I need to know what I should do. I have to tell someone. What if I lie to them and that makes the whole thing go to hell? What if they already know and it makes me look even guiltier? No, I need advice.

"Aiden, I have to tell you something," I say, coming out of the bathroom and launching into what happened today.

Aiden listens carefully without saying a word. Then he goes into the living room and tells Thurston that the meeting for tomorrow is off.

"Please reschedule it," he says when Thurston asks for a clarification. "We need time. A lot more time."

"I'm really not sure if we do," I say. "Maybe I can just tell them what happened."

"Can someone please tell me what's going on?" Thurston demands more than he asks.

"I went to Connecticut today."

"You aren't allowed to leave the state," Thurston says.

"Yes, I know. I'm sorry. But I wanted to go to my friend's gravesite. I had to tell her something important."

"So, you didn't even see a real person?" Thurston gasps. "I mean, a live person?"

"No...but I had to go to her gravesite."

I explain myself further, going over all the reasons that I have just stated to Aiden. Neither of them seem particularly convinced.

"So, you were never going to tell us about it," Aiden says. "If you weren't in a car accident?"

Well, yes, actually that's true, I want to say, but I bite my tongue.

"I'm going to go," Thurston says after a moment. "I'm going to figure this out and get back to you."

As soon as he leaves, I walk up to Aiden and apologize. Again. And again. But he just pushes my hands away from him.

"I'm sorry, okay?" I say. "I'm really, really sorry. I just wanted to have a moment with Caroline. I wasn't sure what was going to happen with this sit-down or whether I was going to go to trial and I needed to talk to her."

"She's dead, Ellie. You can talk to her at any time. You don't have to cross state lines."

"Okay, I know that you believe that, and lots of people do. But it was different to be there. I felt closer to her. I felt her there."

"You just don't get it, do you?" Aiden yells. "You can go away for a very long time. They can put you in prison."

"Don't raise your voice at me," I say. He walks from one side of the room to another. His face is flushed. Steaming. I've never seen him this upset or mad before.

"Don't fucking tell me what to do," he says loudly.

"Well, you don't tell me what to do!" I yell back. My ears start to buzz. Is this really happening? Are we really screaming at each other?

"I need some space," he says, heading toward the front door.

"No, no." I run up to him. "You are not walking out on me. I need to talk to you about this."

"What do you want to talk about?"

"I already apologized, okay? I'm sorry."

Why won't he forgive me? I wonder. Just forgive me. I said that I was sorry.

"What do you want from me?" he asks.

"I want you to stay and talk to me."

"Talk to you about what, exactly? How I'm here doing everything in my power to make sure that nothing happens to you? And you, just run off and break one of the most important conditions of your bail? They are going to take away your bail. You know that? You're going to have to sit in jail until your court date."

"Fuck you!" I yell. Now, it's my turn to walk away. More like run away. I slam the door to the bedroom and lock it. Tears start to run down my cheeks. Hot angry tears.

He is just saying all of those things to hurt me. To scare me. I know that he doesn't mean any of that. He doesn't even know if they will come true. But I'm angry anyway.

There's a knock on the door. I ignore him. He knocks again. This time louder.

"Ellie, please, I'm sorry."

"Fuck you!" I yell through the door.

"I'm sorry, I didn't mean to say that."

I don't say anything.

"Look, I apologized," he says sarcastically. "Why don't you forgive me?"

"Go fuck yourself, Aiden," I say quietly.

He knocks again.

"Please open the door," he pleads in a completely different tone. "Please."

I get off the bed and unlock the door. Before he walks in, I plop back down on the bed and bury my head in the pillows.

"Ellie," he says, sitting down next to me.

"Don't you know that I'm an idiot?" I ask. My voice is muffled by the pillows.

"What?" He pulls on my shoulder. I repeat myself and bury my head in his shoulders.

"I know that I shouldn't have gone there. I know that now. I mean, I had my apprehension about it. But I also didn't know what was going to happen and I wanted to talk to her. One last time."

"Don't talk like that," he says, putting his hand around me. He runs his fingers through my hair, petting my head. "Everything is going to be okay."

"No, it's not," I mumble.

"I'm going to make it okay. I promise."

I inhale and exhale deeply. I don't know if I really believe him, but in this moment I do. I believe him, mainly because I have to. I don't have any other choice. I need this to be okay because I can't imagine it being not okay. What do I have waiting for me on the other end of *not okay*? A trial. A guilty verdict. Having my baby in prison. Never seeing him again. No, that can't happen. No, no, no. Tears start to roll down my cheeks and my whole body starts to shake.

Aiden wraps his hands firmly around me and holds me as I cry.

It takes me more than a few minutes to calm down. The pregnancy is, of course, not helping my overall mood management, but frankly I have no idea how much of my emotional outpour can be attributed to that versus the reality of this situation.

"I'm going to be okay," I say, pulling myself away from Aiden. He lets me go and lies down on the bed, closing his eyes.

I stand up and head to the bathroom. I glance at myself in the mirror. It's not a pretty sight. My eye makeup is all smeared with big black splotches around my cheeks, where I wiped the tears away with the back of my hand. I splash water on my face and wipe off the remnants. Is this really going to be okay? I ask myself, silently staring at my reflection in the mirror. I don't know. I really don't know. But what is there really to do but to take each moment as it comes? I take a deep breath. For now, stop obsessing about it. You need rest and if you keep going back and forth about all the things that you should or shouldn't have done, you won't get any sleep at all. Tomorrow's a new day to make all new decisions. And mistakes. Shit, here I go again. I splash more cold water on my face and put everything that happened out of my mind.

After running a brush through my tangled hair, I pull down my pants and sit down on the toilet. That's when I see all the blood.

CHAPTER 39 - ELLIE

WHEN SOMETHING WORSE HAPPENS...

*T*he blood is everywhere. All over my panties and thighs. I stare at the red liquid for a few moments. Mesmerized. But not in a good way. Why is it here? What's going on? Aren't I not supposed to have my period when I'm pregnant?

Then it hits me. No. No. No. This isn't my period. This is something bad. Very bad.

"Aiden!" I yell. "Aiden! I have to go to the hospital!"

The next hour is a blur. Aiden speeds through the streets to get me to the hospital. He keeps telling me that everything is going to be fine. He is holding my hand. He is right here next to me, but it feels like he's a million miles away. And then the next moment, I see him and hear him, but he's muffled. He's no longer far away, but there's a big wall of plexiglass separating us.

Help me, I say over and over, but nothing comes out of my mouth.

I look over at him. I can't hear anything he's saying either. All I see are bright lights whizzing by me, engulfing me.

The car stops in front of a big red sign. I try to read what it says, but I can't. E. Mer. I look closer. It's like my brain isn't connected to my mind. I should know what it says, but I don't.

Emergency.

Yes, that's right. We're at the emergency entrance to the hospital.

A bunch of people run out. They put me into a wheelchair and roll me into a bright white hallway. I cover my eyes to shield myself from the flood of fluorescent lights.

Aiden is barking orders somewhere behind me.

Nurses and other medical staff gather around me as they wheel me into a room.

———

SOME PEOPLE ARE JUST NOT MEANT to be born. At least, that's one of the theories out there. Some people just don't want to be born. I don't know if this is the case with my son or not. I know that all the doctors and nurses who are milling around me are trying their best to stop this miscarriage from happening. Aiden is, of course, doing his best in giving everyone orders, even those people who don't work for him, and that's pretty much everyone around here.

What am I doing? Nothing really. I'm just lying here in bed, trying to stay perfectly still despite of all the commotion around me. Just breathe, I say to myself over and over. But I'm not just talking to myself. I'm also talking to my son. Just breathe, I say to him. Just stay with me. I will be here for you no matter what.

The thing about surprise babies is that they aren't exactly planned. That seems obvious, but with the surprise comes something else as well. It's this feeling of uncertainty. It's not that I don't want the baby; it's just that I've never really given it much thought. I'm shocked that it happened. So, it's hard to really know how you feel about the whole thing. Until now, that is.

Now, lying here in this hospital bed, I know that I want him. I want him to stay with me. I don't know whether he wants to come into this world. Or whether he will be too good for this world (probably), but I still selfishly want him here.

Please stay, I say to myself. Please stay.

"Please stay," I say out loud. My voice cracks in the middle, but I remain steadfast. "Please stay," I repeat over and over again.

Not long after that, the bleeding stops. Just as mysteriously, and without much of an explanation, as it started. The doctor and the nursing staff are a bit dumbfounded, but they try not to let on. They keep me overnight for observation. They talk to me about what might or might not happen in the future. I wrap my arm around my stomach and listen, taking in what they are saying with a grain of salt.

"Are you okay?" Aiden asks after everyone finally leaves the room. I nod and smile.

"I think it's going to be okay now," I say.

"Really? How do you know?"

"I don't know." I shrug. "I just have a feeling."

He takes my hand and gives it a big squeeze.

"I'm sorry about today," Aiden starts to say, but the door swings open and our moms and Brie appear. It's a bit shocking to see them all in the same place, but I'm too tired to deal with it right now. I decide not to focus on any possible drama, but instead just welcome them in.

"What are you all doing here?" I ask tentatively, looking at Aiden.

"I called them. I wasn't sure what was going to happen and I thought they should know."

"How are you feeling?" Mom and Brie ask almost simultaneously. "What happened?"

I go over the highlights of what happened. They oh and ah and shake their heads. Aiden's mom gives me a little pat on my hand and a smile.

"Do you have good doctors here?" She turns to Aiden and asks.

"Yes," he says.

"Because if not, I have no problem with moving her down to where she can get proper medical care," she says with a wink. It's a joke. And one that makes me smile broadly.

The three of them stay for close to an hour before Aiden finally ushers them out. I can honestly say, with even a hint of sarcasm, I actually had a good time. If he had asked me about them coming here beforehand, I would've told him a categorical no. But when they leave, I'm actually a little bit sad to see them go. Somehow, they all meld well together. I still have my individual issues with both his mom and mine, but when they are both here at the same time, along with Brie, who is always a good sport for brokering any truce, it feels good. Nice, actually. It's good to know that there are people out there who will be here for me. Who love me. And who are here for my son.

"Okay, now that they are gone," Aiden says, closing the door behind them. "I want to ask you something."

CHAPTER 40 - ELLIE

*a*iden takes my hand and gets down on one knee. I shake my head.

"What are you doing?"

"You know what I'm doing."

He looks straight into my eyes and tells me he loves me. He tells me all the things that he has told me before.

"No," I say. "I can't do this again."

"What do you mean?"

"I mean, yes, I want to get married. But we have been engaged before, you know."

"Of course, I know." He nods. I try to turn away, but he walks around the bed.

"Okay, no engagement this time."

"What does that mean?"

He shrugs. "I don't know exactly except that we shouldn't call it an engagement. You're right; we have been engaged before and maybe that's not the best thing for us."

I don't know why I'm pulling away from him, except that I am. Maybe this isn't the best time. Maybe he's not saying the right things. Maybe I've just been through way too much to deal with this right now.

Aiden takes my hand in his. He looks deep into my eyes. There's a severity that comes over him. A darkness. I get a glimpse of the man I saw before. On the yacht.

"Ellie," he says slowly. Deliberately. "You are going to be my wife."

I stare at him. No question. No options. No decisions to be made. What is this feeling that's come over me? It's like all the heaviness is lifted from my shoulders.

"But—" I start to say, but he just puts his finger on my lips.

"I am not asking you. I am telling you."

I nod.

"You are going to have a proper wedding. The thing that bridal magazines are made of. A dream wedding."

I start to feel queasy again. The prospect of making all those decisions. Who to invite. What to wear. Where to have it. Finding just the right venue. I feel my whole body tensing up just at the thought of that. As if he can read my mind, Aiden furrows his brows.

"No," he says.

"What?"

"No. You won't have to plan a thing. It will be perfect and beautiful and everything you ever wanted, but you won't do a thing."

"Really? But how?"

"You'll see."

I like the sound of that. Frankly, I don't really have any opinions about how a wedding should be. The ones featured in the magazines all seem beautiful and good enough. And then, my thoughts drift to something I do want to make a decision about.

"What about my dress?"

"You can pick that out yourself if you want."

"I like that."

Aiden gives me a little smile.

"So, let me get this straight? We are not engaged. And we're going to have a dream wedding, but I won't have to make any decisions about anything?"

"Yes."

"And how is that going to happen?"

"It's going to happen because Mr. Black is going to take care of it for you."

CHAPTER 41 - AIDEN

*T*his time, I don't ask. I mean, I did, but then I changed my mind. There is a well-known psychological fact that having too many choices results in anxiety and unhappiness with the final decision. Ellie has been through a lot. We have been engaged before. We almost got married. I know that she wants to marry me. What she doesn't want to do is think about getting married again. Too much has gone wrong before when she did.

So, my gift to her is to just take the decision out of it. I don't ask the question. I just tell her what's going to happen. As soon as I do, I see a wave of relief sweep over her face. It's the exact thing that she wants. She wants to have it all, but she doesn't want to think about doing it. It's like designing a house. Lots of people like the idea of building an entirely custom-built house, but they don't know how much stress comes with making all of those choices. A much better choice, for some, is to just see a beautiful home that has everything you want and get it instead. That's what I'm going to do for Ellie. She is going to give me the biggest gift of my life. This is the least I can do.

Don't worry though. I'm not going to rely on my personal aesthetic to put together a wedding. I'm going to hire one of the most exclusive wedding planners there is. And she's going to do it. She's going to take care of every last detail. Except for the wedding dress.

"Do you think we can get married at the New York Public Library?" Ellie asks after a moment. "I mean, I know that I'm not supposed to make decisions and all, but it's nostalgic. We had one of our first dates there."

The idea of the place floods me with memories. All the flowers that I brought in for our dinner date at the Celeste Bartos Forum. The party planner pursued me to go for the light pink and purple lighting, which transformed the place into a room of romance and love. It especially drew attention to the thirty-foot high glass saucer ceiling. Come to think of it, that's a great place for a wedding venue. It's nearly sixty-five square feet in space, plenty for a wedding of any size.

"You are not supposed to be making any decisions," I say. "I don't want this to stress you out."

"No, you're right. You're right."

"Unfortunately, I don't think you'll be allowed to go to New York, remember. We have to stay in the state."

"Oh, yes, of course," she says. "I forgot. Okay, never mind. I'll leave it up to you. The wedding you had planned at the garden at the hospital was beyond my dreams, so I know that this one will be as well."

"All you have to know," I say, "is that this wedding will be perfect. With lots of guests we don't really know. With a budget that's way too much and food that's too expensive. And memories that we will never forget."

She laughs. I smile.

"Why are you doing this, Aiden?" she asks after a moment. "I mean, we can easily just go to the courthouse and get it over with."

"Yes, I know. But after everything we've been through, I think our relationship deserves a little celebration. A little too much overindulgence. Besides, it will give us something to look forward to in the midst of all this possible trial shit."

Her face falls. I immediately regret bringing that up. The whole point of this engagement and wedding is to not think about the fact that our life isn't really our own. We don't really know what's going to happen and if the district attorney decides to take this to trial for the publicity, well, who the hell knows what's going to happen.

"You are right. We do need this. Something good to think about. To live life to the fullest, now," Ellie says, pulling herself together and wiping a little tear from the corner of her eye.

CHAPTER 42 - ELLIE

WHEN I LOOK FOR A DRESS…

*T*hurston has done a good job of postponing the meeting with the DA and the detectives for another week. At first I'm, of course, relieved. Happy to have more time.

But then it just makes me even more anxious. Instead of being figured out, and dealing with the consequences, the whole thing is just getting dragged out. The only way I can really cope with not knowing is by putting the whole thing out of my mind. I try to stay busy. Occupy my hands and mind. The best way to do that is to write.

Aiden and I return to the hotel and while he works from the living room, I make myself at home on the large California King bed and dig into the last book

of my story. Everything is coming to an end. It's
bittersweet. I don't want to leave them, but I want
them to get their happily ever after. My readers keep
asking me when the last book will be out and I
decide that this week will be the week that I finally
finish it.

The one thing that I know is that they deserve their
happy ending because I don't know if I will get one.
Aiden is planning this amazing wedding for us, but
it feels more like a going away party. Most people are
excited for their big day because it's the beginning of
their lives together. But me? I don't know if I'm even
going to be around next year. I mean, what if the
worst happens? What if they decide to take this to
trial and the jury finds me guilty? What then?
Shivers run down my spine.

No, you can't think like that. Stay positive, Ellie.
That's not going to happen. But is this even a good
thing to think? Maybe I should prepare myself for
the worst, just because it's a possibility? Then I will
be more prepared. I feel sick to my stomach. How do
you even prepare to go to prison for a crime you
didn't commit? I mean, I did kill him, but it was all in
self-defense.

No, I'm not going to think like that. If the worst happens, I will need to fight this. I will need all of my strength to fight for my life. Preparing for doing time is not an option. Especially, now that I have my baby on the way and a husband-to-be. I turn my attention back to the screen and begin writing. No matter what happens, these people that my readers fell in love with are going to have the best ending possible. Their love story is going to be one for the ages. It's going to be one that people will want to read over and over again.

After writing for more than two hours with total focus, in an almost fever-like state, I give Aiden a peck on the lips and head out to my bridal appointment at Monique's. It's the best bridal boutique store in all of Boston, according to Aiden's wedding planner. On my way over, I pop into a Starbucks and buy a large chocolate chip muffin. It's not the best thing, but I am pregnant. Really pregnant and really hungry. Now that the nausea is somewhat controlled with the pills, I am still tired all the time and, on top of that, I'm also hardly ever satiated. As soon as I finish breakfast, I'm already thinking of lunch. My stomach starts to make noises and I have to have something, otherwise, I'm just going to feel sick again.

I arrive at the boutique feeling very guilty and unhappy with my body. This is definitely not an attitude that's very conducive to bridal gown shopping. I know that, of course. But that's life, huh?

The woman who meets me is dressed in a very sensible black suit and heels. Her hair is pulled out of her face and her makeup is flawless, but minimal. In the soothing, effervescent voice of a smooth jazz radio DJ, she introduces herself as Azelia and asks me what kind of outlines I prefer.

"I don't really know," I say. "I just need something that will fit me in a few weeks. I am going to be seven months pregnant at this wedding."

"Oh, wow, congratulations," she says without batting an eye. Hopefully, I am not the only knocked up bride that she has had the pleasure to dress.

"Well, then, how about we start with an empire waist? They are very flattering and will give your stomach room to expand."

She takes me to a large room lined on all sides with

luxurious drapery. There's a three piece mirror in the middle. She tells me to wait here as she picks out some dresses for me to try on.

I take off my coat and finish the rest of my tea. I stuff the last bit of the muffin and lick my fingers. Man, Aiden is marrying a class act here, I say, looking at myself in the mirror.

I know that everyone nowadays preaches the importance of self-love and appreciating the body that you have. The only problem with that is how to actually get there. I look at myself in the mirrors. I haven't really gained that much weight, but I have a small frame and I feel huge. Plus, it's not so much that I feel fat (can I even say that anymore? Is that appropriate? But aren't I entitled to the feelings that I have?). It's more that I feel puffy. It's like my whole body just got inflamed, or is it engorged? My breasts do look better, which is hard to complain about. But why did my arms have to get big, too? And my face? The problem is just there's just too much flesh.

"Okay, I found this one for you," Azelia says. "Now, when your fiancé called, he made it very clear that there is no budget. Is that correct?"

"Oh, I didn't know that."

"You lucky, lucky woman," Azelia says. "I can't tell you how many women come here to try on their dream dress and their dream dress is always two or three thousand above their set aside budget."

I'm sure that's more of a problem for you than for them, I want to say. But I keep my mouth shut. This woman is just trying to be nice. I shouldn't take out my bad mood on her.

"Okay, to be honest, I'm a bit out of my element here," I say. "But is there really such a big difference between one dress and another? I mean, I've seen dresses that cost like seven thousand. That's crazy to me."

Azelia stares at me with an appalled look on her face.

"We have dresses here that cost one hundred and seven thousand," she says. "And if you can afford them, they are worth every penny."

Now, it's my turn to be appalled. My mouth actually drops open like I'm in some sort of cartoon.

"Here, come here," she says. "Follow me."

She leads me out of the room, down a long hallway, and into another large room. This is a room of wedding dresses. There are hundreds of them, each one hanging in its own see-through zipped up garment bag. I don't know how anyone can find anything in here. There are tags on the top, but other than that it's just a sea of different shades of white.

Azelia pulls out one dress and shows me the material. "You see the stitching here and the beading here. It's gorgeous, right?"

I nod. I've never seen something so delicate before. The pictures in the bridal magazines don't do it justice.

"It's all done by hand, of course," she explains. "Well, this dress is only twelve thousand. Now, follow me, and I'll show you one that costs eighty-nine."

She takes me into a smaller room. Here the dresses are hanging a bit apart from each other. The lighting is more soothing as well. Not as bright.

"All the dresses here, cost over thirty," she explains. "Now, look at the beading here."

She pulls out a dress at the far corner. Up close, the

difference is like night and day. The beading is exquisite. It covers nearly the entire corset and goes down the sides. The stitching is even more precise, if that's the right word. It's hard to explain exactly except to say this looks like a dress that belongs in a museum.

"You see, the dresses that cost this much, they are basically works of art. They come with their own people who will make the dress fit you just right. They can be altered in many different ways. Everything about them is hand-made with only the best fabrics."

I nod. Now, I understand. Maybe not fully understand, but I have an idea.

"And these dresses?" I ask when we get back to my dressing room. "The ones you picked out? Are they fancy or works of art?"

She smiles. "Your fiancé also told me to not tell you how much it is. He wants you to pick it because you love it."

"Was he seriously worried that I would pick the most expensive dress there is just because?" I ask, furrowing my brows. That doesn't sound like Aiden. Not at all.

"No, he thought that you would pick a dress that was the cheapest just because it was," she explains.
I laugh.

"Don't worry. I brought a selection here. Different types and styles of empire waists. We can also try other ones as well, if you like."

CHAPTER 43- ELLIE

*A*fter three hours of trying on dresses, my head is starting to swim. When I tried on the first one, I was certain that that was the one I had to have, but Azelia insisted that I try on another one and then things got more complicated. They are all gorgeous, of course. But some are just not my style.

"I think I might call it a day," I say after a moment. "I might have to come back."

"Why don't you take a little break?" she says. "I can have some lunch brought in."

"Oh, no, that's not necessary. Not at all," I say. It will just be too weird to have lunch brought in for me. I mean, I'm not this fancy person at all, despite the fact that I'm shopping here of all places.

She gets a serious expression on her face. "Ellie, please don't leave. Aiden arranged for a surprise for you. I don't want to ruin it, but it's not going to happen for another twenty minutes."

"O-kay," I say slowly.

"So, how about that lunch?"

While Azelia goes to put in the order for an avocado toast and a greens smoothie, I am left all alone with all of my options. Much to my surprise, my mind doesn't immediately go to worrying about the surprise that Aiden has arranged. Instead, I close my eyes and imagine myself walking down the aisle in one of these dresses.

I clear my mind. I breathe in and out. And then I see myself walking toward Aiden. Suddenly, the decision disappears completely. It's no longer a decision. There's only one way to go. One right dress for the occasion. All the other ones aren't even contenders.

"Azelia!" I yell down the hall. "I'd like to try the first dress on again."

She helps me into it. As soon as I feel it against my body, I know that it's the right one. It has a whimsical neckline which Azelia refers to as 'illusion' and a high empire waist. It's floor length and has a long sweeping train. The white silk Chantilly lace gown comes with embroidery overlay and a silk white embroidered overskirt. This time, when I look at my reflection in the mirror, tears start to flow down my face.

"This is the one," I say.

Azelia covers her mouth with her hand, also overcome with emotion. "You look absolutely beautiful," she whispers before excusing herself.

I enjoy the one-on-one time I have with my dress. I stand here, admiring it from every direction. A few minutes pass and then another few. I don't actually want to take it off. Suddenly, I wish I could do everything in this dress.

When Azelia comes back, she asks me to come outside of the room with her. It will be nice to see the dress in a different setting, I think, excited to have it on for a little bit longer.

"Oh my God." I hear my mom's distinct voice gasp. All three of them crowd around me, wanting to give me a hug, but not wanting to do anything to damage the dress. Eventually, we settle with air kisses and distant hugs where only our arms intertwine without our bodies touching.

"You look absolutely gorgeous," Brie says.

"You do," Mom says.

"Ellie, you are breathtaking," Arlene, Aiden's mother, says. Whatever tension might have existed between me and either my mom and me and Arlene doesn't in this moment. Right now, everything is perfect. I can see how happy they are for me and how much they all love me.

I twirl around. I can't help myself. Once I stand on my tiptoes and give my body a little spin, everything starts to move on its own. It's almost as if the dress has a life of its own.

"You look amazing," Brie says, colliding into me once I get a bit dizzy and slow down. She grabs me by my shoulders and gives me a big warm hug. When she pulls away, I can see tears in the corners of her eyes.

Wow, Brie, of all people. She is not one to give in to her emotions easily. I'm actually shocked.

"Is this the dress?" she asks. I nod.

As I gaze into my reflection in the mirror, I hear Arlene turn to my mom and say, "She is the most beautiful bride I've ever seen."

After close to a half an hour of admiring myself, even I've had enough. Azelia follows me back to the dressing room to help me get out of the dress.

"Your family seems pleased," she says.

I nod. "I'm actually surprised."

"Really? Why?"

"Well, besides my sister, things haven't exactly been smooth sailing with Arlene and me. Or my mom and me."

"Weddings have a way of bringing people together," Azelia says.

"I guess. Still, I'm surprised they came at all."

"Mr. Black arranged for it."

"Yeah, I figured," I say as she pulls the dress off me. Once I'm out, I'm left standing in just a slip, which is also quite nice. In a different decade, like the 90s, this would be a dress all on its own.

"Hey, can I ask you something?"

"Anything," Azelia says.

"I got the feeling that you knew which dress I was going to pick."

Azelia nods.

"You did? How did you know?"

"I always know," she says with a shrug. "You can always see it on the bride's face when she's found her dress."

"What do you mean?"

"All anxiety and nervousness seem to vanish immediately. They get this placid, almost sedate look on their faces. You did as well. And then when I take them out into the main room to look at themselves in the large mirror, they often burst out in tears."

"Wow, what a clinical explanation of what I just experienced in there," I joke.

"Just because an experience is not unique doesn't mean that it's not special," she says. "Everyone falls in love. The broad strokes of the story are pretty similar if you don't account for the details. But it's the details that make each individual love story unique and special in a way that no other one can ever be. It's unique to each individual couple and that specific time and place in history when they fell in love."

Her words touch my heart. She's right. Of course, she's right. Almost everyone falls in love in their life, at least I hope so. It's one of the most commonplace things that has ever happened and will ever happen to a person on earth. And yet, each story is unique. I would say utterly unique, but there are no degrees of uniqueness. That's why love stories are so fascinating. The ebbs and flows of romance is what keeps the world turning because what greater motivation is there in this universe than love. What's the point of anything without love?

CHAPTER 44 - ELLIE

The next few weeks pass quickly even though I don't do any of the wedding planning. To make sure that I'm not too pregnant for our wedding, Aiden and I decided to have the ceremony on the twenty-ninth week of my pregnancy. Seven months. Ideally, I wouldn't have been pregnant at all because the thought of being a bride is nauseating enough, but being this far along was definitely better than earlier in my pregnancy. It was better, even though I was much bigger and rather unwieldy.

Ever since I picked up my dress, I try on my dress every other day. I want to make sure that it still fits. It

does, and every time I try it on, I feel beautiful. I
don't know what it is about a particular piece of
clothing, especially just the right dress, but it
somehow has the power to change how you feel
about yourself. I woke up tired and hungover, even
though I haven't had a drink since I found out I was
pregnant, and sick to my stomach. As soon as I
brush my teeth, wash my face, and put on some
makeup, I head to the closet and put on the dress. It's
silly really, but I figure that I'm only going to
officially wear this dress once, so why not wear it a
bunch of times unofficially.

Finally, it's the day of my wedding. Aiden and I
spend the night before apart, just to make the next
night a little more special. He got another suite at
our hotel and he will be waiting for me at the venue
at four o'clock. I'm a little bummed that we can't
have our wedding at the place where we had our first
real date, but I try not to think about it. Whatever
Aiden and the wedding planner put together is
probably ten times better.

Brie arrives around eleven to help me get ready.
She's my maid of honor, though that's not the title
that either of us have used. Brie is still going through

a lot. We haven't talked about it much, but she is still going through a bit of a transition. She is no longer interested in being called a 'she', but she isn't quite ready to be referred to as a 'he' either. I'm supposed to use the pronoun 'they,' it's non-gender binary. It's the right thing to say, but I keep forgetting. Well, not in real life. Just when I think about her in my own personal thoughts. For now, she is still a 'she' to me.

As the makeup artist cleanses my face, I turn to Brie and say, "I know that we haven't talked about this for a while, but how is everything going with your...changes."

"Fine, I guess," she says.

"Oh, I'm sorry," I say, suddenly realizing that the makeup artist is here. "I forgot. We don't have to talk about this now."

"No, it's nothing like that," Brie says, examining her face in the mirror. "In case you were wondering, I'm transitioning."

"Oh, to a man?" the makeup artist asks nonchalantly.

"Yes," Brie nods.

"Wow, how exciting."

Hmm, maybe she does have a point. Maybe this transition thing doesn't have to be scary at all. I mean, I was feeling weird about it, but why do I have to? I mean, Brie is still Brie. So, what if I had a sister for a while? Now, I'll have a brother. But they'll still be Brie.

"I'm here for you, Brie, you know that, right?" I say. "If you want to talk about this."

"Thank you. I appreciate that. But you probably don't want to talk about this on your wedding day."

"Actually, this is the exact thing I want to talk about," I say. "You know how uncomfortable I am with all eyes on me. It's kind of nice to have someone else's drama to focus on."

"You mean, you don't want to have your big day?"

"I am having a big day. A huge party. But we're also just sitting here, hanging out, talking. I want to talk about you. It will take my mind off all the scary parts that are coming up, like walking down the aisle with everyone's eyes on me."

Brie smiles and shakes her head. "You're unbelievable, Ellie. Here you are marrying a billionaire, seven months pregnant, getting ready for your wedding, and all you want to talk about is me and my stupid problems."

"It's not as selfless as you think," I say. "I like gossip."

Everything I say in that moment is true. I do like gossip. And I do want to take my mind off this wedding, which is just making my stomach turn in knots.

"I've decided that I would like to transition," Brie says. "I definitely don't identify as as a woman anymore. I'm not sure if I want to go all the way and become a full man, biologically speaking, but for now my gender is non-binary."

"So, the pronoun 'they' is appropriate?" I ask.

"Yes." She nods. "And before you ask, I'm into men and women."

"I'm glad," I say.

"Really?"

"Yep. I mean, this way you have a better chance of finding someone who can put up with you," I joke.

Brie rolls her eyes.

Just as my makeup is ready, Mom walks in without a knock.

CHAPTER 45 - ELLIE

WHEN WE GET READY…

*M*om comes in carrying four cups of coffee with her - for her, us, and Arlene - and I can feel anxiety emanating from her.

"Oh my God, there's still so much to do," she says, handing us our cups. "Arlene's not here yet? Where is she?"

"Mom, calm down," I say, even though I know that that's the last thing that's going to make her calm.

"I can't! It's my daughter's wedding day!"

"What is it that you have to do?" Brie asks. "Isn't the wedding planner taking care of everything?"

"Yes, but I still have to get my makeup done and put on my dress," she says quickly.

"So, that's like two things," Brie says. "You can do that in twenty minutes and you have four hours."

"And my hair!" Mom says. "Besides, there are a lot of details to worry about. I mean, what if—"

"Mom, calm down," I say in my most stern voice. "You don't have to worry. That's what the wedding planner is here for. She will worry about the details."

I swear to God, worrying is like my mom's primary job. It's no wonder she can't get much else done. It's practically all she does.

"Don't tell me not to worry. I'm a mother. Once you become one, you'll know what it's like."

We'll see about that. My mom has the tendency to say stuff like that. You'll know when you get older. You'll know when you get to college. You'll know when you get married. The typical cliché kind of stuff, which is only sometimes true. But the truth is that I'm a bit of a worrier and a fretter, but not at all like her. And when I do let my thoughts get away from me, I always try to pull myself back. Yes, crazy things happen all the time. But worrying about things you don't have control of isn't going to really make everything much better.

The irony of these thoughts isn't lost on me, of course. Don't think that. I have spent more than a few restless nights worrying about possibly going away for life for killing a man in self-defense. But that seems like an actually legit thing to worry about, unlike this wedding.

"Mom, how about this?" Brie says. "How about I give you something else to think about?"

I glance over at her. She's waiting for my okay. I smile and nod.

"Mom, I no longer identify as a woman," she says firmly. There is wavering in her words this time, unlike the time when she said this to me.

Mom stares at her dumbfounded just as Arlene comes in. My smile just gets wider. This is the most perfect thing that could happen on my wedding day, and I'm saying that without a tinge of sarcasm.

"If you talk about me, I'd like you to refer to me by my name or the pronoun 'they.' I am in transition, but I'm not sure if I want to become a man. I will not answer any questions about sexual re-assignment surgery, so don't even ask. And I've had relationships with both men and women so I consider myself queer."

A photographer comes in right after Arlene and takes a few pictures of us. I have a wide toothy grin on my face mostly as a result of the pride that I feel for my sister right now. Some of it can also be contributed to the shocked expression on my mom's face. I'm glad that the photographer is here to capture the moment. It's not one that I'm going to forget any time soon.

"Why are you telling me this? Why are you ruining your sister's big day?" Mom finally gasps after she regains her ability to speak.

"Because I haven't in a long time. Ellie knows already. She's okay with it."

"But you didn't have to ruin her day!"

"Brie's not ruining my day, Mom. Not at all. Brie has been wanting to tell you this for quite some time, and I'm glad that it finally happened today."

"Why? Did she want to ruin my day?"

"Mom, this isn't about you," Brie says. "This is about me, don't you see that?"

As I watch my mom trying to process this whole thing, I can't help but be a little relieved over the fact that she's no longer freaking out about my wedding. Her level of general anxiety has always been very difficult for me to live with and I'm glad that her present freak-out is actually as a result of something legitimate for once.

A few hours later, after a big lunch and a decent amount of champagne, Mom and Brie are friends again. I'm glad that Arlene is here because she actually managed to put my mom at ease over the whole Brie thing. Actually, I'm shocked by how accommodating and kind she's being. I haven't forgotten what happened when Aiden was in a coma, but a wedding day is not the time to hold on to grudges.

"Okay, it's time to go," I say, glancing at my phone. Everyone stands up and takes one last look at themselves in the mirror. They all look beautiful. My mom is dressed in a flowing lilac dress which is a complement to Arlene's caramel floral dress. Brie is dressed in a sophisticated pant suit, which accentuates her waist and ridiculously long legs, making her look like a runway model. Finally, I look at myself in the mirror as my mom pins my veil.

Everyone inhales simultaneously when I ask them what they think.

"Stunning."

"Gorgeous."

"Absolutely beautiful."

Yes, I think this will do, I say to myself.

CHAPTER 46 - AIDEN

WHEN SHE WALKS DOWN THE AISLE

*T*he wedding planner and her team did an excellent job of setting up the venue. Since neither of us are particularly religious, I decided to skip a church wedding and instead have it at the Old South Meeting House. It's one of the oldest venues in town and remains largely unchanged from 1729 when it was built. As one of the most important Colonial landmarks, the inside looks a lot like a simple white Protestant church or an old style courthouse. It's arranged in the traditional New England meeting house style. It has simplicity of line and symmetrical proportions, which give a quiet, elegant type of beauty that I hope Ellie will love.

I am standing at the end of the aisle with the officiant. The wooden benches inside the meeting house are adorned with flowers. Most of the flowers are daisies and daffodils, Ellie's favorite. They are not fancy or imported, but they are her favorite and they are a perfect complement to this understated setting. Just as the guests are all settling in their seats, my heart jumps into my throat. My thoughts drift back to the last time I was waiting for her at the end of the aisle. And then the doors in the back open and the music starts. Brie comes down the aisle. There's a brief pause while she takes her place across from me. I hold my breath. And then I see her.

Ellie appears at the far end of the aisle. She looks effervescent walking toward me. It's almost as if she is sailing toward me. As she inches closer, my breath gets caught at the back of my throat. Is this really my bride? Bathed in candlelight, she arrives at her place next to me a goddess.

I take her hand in mine and we turn to look at the officiant. Since I did not want to put any more pressure on Ellie than necessary, we did not write our own vows. I knew that she would not want to, so I didn't even ask. Instead, I chose wedding vows out of the Buddhist tradition. After reading over all the vows from various religions, these are the ones that spoke the most to me.

The officiant says the vows and asks me to repeat.

"I, Aiden Black, take you, Ellie Rhodes, to be my wife, my partner in life, and my one true love. I will cherish our friendship and love you today, tomorrow, and forever. I will trust you and honor you. I will laugh with you and cry with you. Through the best and the worst, through the difficult and the easy. Whatever may come, I will always be there. As I have given you my hand to hold so I give you my life to keep."

Through the veil, I can see tears appear in Ellie's eyes. One breaks free and rolls down her cheek. The officiant asks Ellie to make the same vow to me and she does, no longer fighting back tears.

"Recognizing that the external conditions in life will not always be smooth and that internally your own minds and emotions will sometimes get stuck in negativity," the officiant says. "Do you pledge to see all these circumstances as a challenge to help you grow, to open your hearts, to accept yourselves, and each other; and to generate compassion for others who are suffering? Do you pledge to avoid becoming narrow, closed, or opinionated, and to help each other to see various sides of situations?"

She squeezes my hand and we both say, "We do."

"Understanding that just as we are a mystery to ourselves, each other person is also a mystery to us. Do you pledge to seek to understand yourselves, each other, and all living beings, to examine your own minds continually and to regard all the mysteries of life with curiosity and joy?"

Now, I squeeze her hand as we say, "We do."

"Do you pledge to preserve and enrich your affection for each other, and to share it with all beings? To take the loving feelings you have for one another and your vision of each other's potential and inner beauty as an example and rather than spiraling inward and becoming self-absorbed, to radiate this love outward to all beings?"

We squeeze each other's hands simultaneously as we say, "We do."

"Now, repeat after me, in unison," the officiant says.

I look into Ellie's eyes and suddenly we are all alone in the room. The entire outside world falls away and disappears completely.

"Knowing how deeply our lives intertwine with each other and with all beings, we undertake the practice of protecting life," we say at the same time. "Knowing how deeply our lives intertwine with each other and with all beings, we undertake the practice of taking only what is offered. Knowing how deeply our lives intertwine with each other and with all beings, we undertake the practice of cultivating loving-kindness and honesty as the basis for speaking."

"I now pronounce you husband and wife, and you may kiss each other."

I lift up her veil and peer into those dark understanding eyes that see me like the man I only hope I can become. I run my fingers along her jaw and pull her closer to me. When our lips touch, I lose all sense of time and place. Then I see fireworks.

Just as I'm about to pull away, she kisses me again. Pushing herself closer to me, she whispers, "I love you always and forever."

The rest of the wedding is a blur. The wedding planner did a good job in making it look like a dream wedding, good enough for a bridal magazine. We sign our marriage license and we are introduced as husband and wife to the reception guests. Cocktail hour and the reception are held at the Four Seasons hotel ballroom not far from the wedding venue. We dance, and eat, and twirl the night away. We cut the cake and kiss each other on command whenever anyone makes a toast or clinks glasses. I resist the temptation to mush the cake into her face and ruin her makeup, but I know that it's not really the sort of thing that she would like. No matter how much I try to enjoy each moment of this special day, all I can think about is to just be alone with Ellie once again. And it's not that I just want sex. It's more than that. I want everyone else to go away. I want it to just be her and me.

CHAPTER 48 - ELLIE

AFTER THE I DO'S...

*T*he partying lasts way into the night. I've never been to a wedding that went past eleven because the venue was only rented until then, but this one just keeps going and going. Despite the fact that I don't know many of the invited guests, they are friends and colleagues of Aiden's, along with his parents' and my parents' friends and acquaintances, that doesn't stop me from having a good time. Around two in the morning, I take off my heels and continue dancing barefoot. Aiden is here with me every step of the way.

Dancing the night away to one of the most common and strangest choices for a wedding song out there,

Gloria Gaynor's *I Will Survive*, I start to laugh watching Aiden mouthing the words along with me.

"I don't want this night to end!" I yell on top of my lungs, so that he can hear me over the music.

"Me either," he says.

"How long do you think the party will go on?"

"As long as the bride and groom are here."

"You know, just because we leave the dance floor, it doesn't mean that the night will end," he says coyly, taking me by my waist. I smile at him and take a few steps away as the song goes into its chorus.

"What do you mean?" I ask coyly.

"I hear our bridal suite calling us," he says as he twirls me away from him and then back toward him.

After close to forty minutes of goodbyes, we leave the party while it's still going strong. As Aiden leads me upstairs to our penthouse, he wraps his arms around me.

"Thank you," I say. "For planning this beautiful wedding. For marrying me. For everything."

"Thank you for being there for me. And for bringing happiness into my life."

And suddenly, in this quiet moment on the elevator, I feel at peace. My life feels complete. Full. The man of my dreams is my husband. He loves me as much as I love him and that means everything will be okay. Right?

I know that I will follow him wherever he will take me. He doesn't need my permission, not that he ever did. I don't know what the future will hold, but tonight he leads me inside the room and straight toward the bedroom.

Putting his arms around my lower back, he turns me around to face him. His eyes turn a deeper shade without giving that familiar mysterious quality that I've fallen in love with. He brushes his fingers along my bottom lip. His fingertips feel both rough and soft at the same time. He leans closer to me, his breaths colliding with my face. Each breath is like its own kiss, kind and sweet and yet dangerous. After everything that we have been through, we are still standing here. More in love and more in lust than ever before.

Aiden tilts my head slightly to the side. He buries his fingers in my hair. Our lips touch and I see flashes of light. Every part of my body is giving off sparks in anticipation.

As he pushes me down on the bed, our tongues collide. His feels foreign, yet familiar at the same time. One kiss turns into the next, making the hairs on the back of my neck stand up. Slowly, his lips start to make their way down my neck.

My stomach feels a bit heavy and cumbersome and I have to lie on my side to fully enjoy the moment. After I adjust my position, Aiden runs his hands down my back and then back up to my shoulders. Shivers run down my thighs and up my arms. I open my legs a little bit wider.

"What do you want?" I ask. "Do you want something kinky?"

Aiden shakes his head, kissing my collarbone. "No, not tonight," he says. "Unless you do."

I shrug.

"Tonight, I just want to make love to my wife," he says, unzipping the back of my dress. With my corset

undone, my breasts pop right out and into
his mouth.

"Mmmm," he whispers, licking my nipples. I moan
from pleasure and in anticipation of what's to come.

"If this is how you make love to your wife, I'll
take it."

"You haven't seen nothing yet."

Suddenly, the tone of his kisses changes. Before they
were soft and careful, but suddenly, they are forceful
and unapologetic. They become bordering on pain,
but the good kind. Each one sends electric impulses
through my body. Zap. Zap. Zap.

Towering over me, he pulls off my dress. It slides off
without much struggle, leaving me in my panties
and bulging belly. He kneels down over me and
kisses my belly button.

"I don't have that quite flat belly anymore," I say.

"I know." He kisses me along my panty line. "But you
will later. And even if you don't, this is the most
beautiful belly I've ever seen."

I blush at the compliment. All this time later, after

everything we have been through, Aiden Black is still capable of making me blush. It's a bit hard to believe.

As he undresses, I watch as each one of his muscles tenses and relaxes. His six pack glistens in the twilight and I run my fingers over each individual bulge. I can't help but lick my lips.

"Like what you see?"

"Yes." I nod. "It looks delicious."

Through his pants, I can see the girth and the substantial size of his cock. I run my fingers over it and pull Aiden closer to me.

His hands make their way down my body with expert precision. My legs fall open on their own after he pulls off my panties and he slides in between. Aiden slides his hands back, across the curves of my hips, and up my hipbones.

He runs his tongue along the inside of my thighs and inhales me. I get even more wet than I was before. My body rises and falls with each kiss. I pull my legs closed to try to stop myself from getting too aroused, but it's too late.

As Aiden continues to tease me, my mouth dries up, along with all moisture in my body. I tilt my head back and Aiden continues to play with me.

"Oh, Ellie," Aiden moans. I like the way he says my name. It's comforting and sexy all at the same time.

After giving me one long, wet kiss in between my thighs, he pulls himself up and climbs on top of me. He's about to thrust himself inside of me when he changes his mind. A moment later, he is lying behind me. Cradling me. Sliding inside of me, I feel him fill me up. The area in between my legs is begging for him. I don't think I've ever been so wet before.

"I crave you," he whispers. "I love you."

I let out a moan of pleasure.

He moves swiftly and elegantly. After a few thrusts, we are moving as one. Dancing an invisible dance. My feet start to tingle and I know that I'm getting close. I point my toes. Electricity courses through my veins.

"Oh, Aiden," I moan, biting the edge of the sheet. A wave of pleasure comes over me and I hear him moan my name. His movements speed up the closer he gets, driving me wild.

"Ellie! Ellie!" he yells in my ear. A few moments later, he stops moving and collapses into me. I turn around to face him and snuggle up against his powerful and protective body. I close my eyes and relax. Everything is going to be okay. I just know it.

CHAPTER 50 - ELLIE

WHEN WE HAVE A SIT-DOWN...

The only thing that would make my wedding more perfect is a dream honeymoon somewhere where the water is crystal clear and the sand is as white as snow. Unfortunately, real life isn't like that. The thing that awaits me not long after the wedding is that sit-down with the Assistant DA and the main detective along with who knows who else. But they are the main people who will be sitting in judgement and deciding whether this case will indeed go to trial.

Thurston and the rest of my legal team have postponed the sit-down for as long as possible. In fact, it has been more than a few weeks. Luckily, the

DA himself postponed the meeting a full month because of another trial that he was prosecuting. Well, here we are. It's finally here. The morning of.

Luckily, the meeting is scheduled for one in the afternoon. I'm not a morning person in my normal life, but this pregnancy has really taken it out of me. I spend most mornings sleeping in until well past nine and then walking around in a daze for close to an hour as I try to do anything to keep the nausea at bay. This morning is no different except that I have the strong suspicion that my bout of morning sickness has something to do with possible doom, which may result from the sit-down.

"You're going to be fine. Everything's going to be fine," Aiden keeps saying over and over. He's pacing the room. Cracking his knuckles. Drinking about five cups of coffee. All signs that everything is not alright. I've never seen him this nervous before. And the more he tries to cover his tracks, the more obvious his anxiety becomes.

When I'm finally ready, I glance at myself one last time in the mirror. I'm wearing a flowing above the knee floral dress. It's business casual and maternity, of course, since it's thirty-nine weeks today. At first, I thought about going for a traditional gray suit with a pencil skirt. You know, the works. But it was so uncomfortable to sit in that I had to go with something that gave my body room to breathe. I have no idea how long this meeting will go for, but I have to be comfortable. At least, as comfortable as possible.

"Aiden, no matter what happens today, it's going to be fine," I say.

"What do you mean?"

"I've decided to make it so. No matter what. What I mean is that we will get through this."

This makes him feel a little better and that in turn makes me feel better, too. Maybe I can get through this with just some positive thinking.

We arrive at a nondescript office building downtown fifteen minutes before our appointment. Someone shows us inside and toward the right office. It's a large conference room with a big view of the city through the wall-to-wall windows along the far side. I hope that I get to sit on the side facing the view.

As soon as we come in, everyone introduces themselves. All the names get jumbled together except for two. Thomas Mann, the Assistant District Attorney, is a large intimidating man in his late forties. He has a big frame and about fifty additional pounds on him. He sits directly across from me at the conference table and buries his head in paperwork. His appearance is somewhat disheveled, almost sweaty.

He whispers something to the guy next to him as I shake Detective Egan's hand. The DA is asking him something about another case. His words are frantic and disoriented. I can't quite make out what he's saying, but it doesn't sound good. It sounds like their case is falling apart.

"I thought that we were going to see Detective—" Thurston starts to say, but Detective Egan interrupts him.

"I've taken over the case from him," he explains. "He has taken a leave of absence."

I was wondering why Egan didn't look familiar. I thought that too much time had passed or I didn't have a great memory of him before, but I guess not.

Getting even more agitated and flustered, Mann excuses himself for a few moments. We all sit here in silence until he comes back.

"Okay, let's get this over with," he says when he comes back. "I don't have much time. Everything in New York seems to be falling apart without me."

My heart skips a beat. I thought that I would have time to explain, to make my case. I glance over at Thurston, who shrugs his shoulders lightly. Someone turns on the camera. They place me under oath.

"I've reviewed your case," Mann says, finally looking up at me from the file. "Carefully."

"Okay," I mumble. Thurston nudges me. I'm supposed to be more forceful. Confident. We had talked about this in our prep. But right now I just feel meek and scared.

"If you had reviewed my file, then you should be well aware of the fact that what happened at my apartment was pure self-defense," I say, sitting up straight. The words escape my lips just as we had practiced them.

"Yeah, yeah," Mann mumbles. "But you see here, there's the issue of your online journal where you clearly state that you want to kill Blake."

"Yes, so what?" I say, shrugging my shoulders. I'm trembling inside, but on the outside I'm calm and collected. Arrogant even. I'm challenging his authority with my gaze.

"You don't think that's a little strange?"

"Not at all. That man ruined my husband's business. He got him fired. He almost forced himself on me, nearly raping me. And then he attacked my husband and put him in a coma, Mr. Mann," I say. "I've had a lot of reasons to want him dead and I vented about that in my private online journal."

"Don't you think that's just a little bit convenient though?"

"Not at all." I shrug. Nonchalance is my motto. "I'm a writer, as I'm sure you know. We all express ourselves in different ways. I express myself in my writing. That's all I was doing."

"I see."

"I wasn't planning anything, if that's what you are

insinuating. My only plan was to never see him again and to get him out of our lives forever. But I never wanted to kill him. And then he came into my apartment and attacked me. I did what anyone in my position would do."

CHAPTER 51 - ELLIE

Time seems to stand still in this conference room. Every moment is carefully tracked and monitored. Not by any of them, but by me. Every moment lasts a lifetime. Mr. Mann looks me up and down, narrowing his eyes.

"I see that you are not fully convinced," I say.

"I have my reservations."

I take a deep breath. I have to try harder. I have to make him understand.

"I killed him with a pen, Mr. Mann." My cool and collected nature is starting to fade away.

"Yes, it appears as though you did."

"Well, there are a lot more powerful weapons out there than pens. And if I were planning something like that, I certainly wouldn't use something like that when he had a gun."

Mr. Mann considers this for a moment, as if he hadn't thought about this before. Of course, he did. I know it. We all know it. Nothing new is going to be revealed in this meeting. The only reason we are all here is for him to evaluate me. If he wants to take this to trial then I have to be unsympathetic. A porn-writing temptress as my first attorney saw me. So, it's my job to persuade him that I am not this person at all and that the jury will not see me this way.

"Mr. Mann, what can I do?" I ask after a moment of silence.

"What do you mean?"

"What can I do to convince you that I didn't do this on purpose? That I was just acting in self-defense?"

Mr. Mann turns his head toward Detective Egan. They talk in hushed tones. We all wait.

"Mr. Mann," Thurston says after waiting for one of them to say something for a while without so much as a word. "What we have here is a young woman who was attacked by a man with a gun. A man who had it out for her husband and her. He was unstable. She did what anyone in her position would do."

"I'm sorry, but given the nature of the journals that we found, I am not so sure that it's that simple," he says after a moment.

My heart sinks. I thought that we were making progress. I thought that this might finally come to an end.

"Ellie, may I speak frankly?" Mr. Mann says.

Just as I nod, wetness spreads down my legs. I get a shooting pain in my back. Oh my god. No. What's happening? I try to stay calm. It's going to be okay, I say to myself. Everything's going to be okay. I just have to get through this.

"I know that you had your issues with the victim, but the details of your online entries do not make you a very sympathetic defendant. And that's before I even tell the jury what you do for a living."

"I didn't plan on this," I say, my voice going up at the end. I'm getting desperate. I'm breaking character.

But I'm going into labor and my back is hurting like the worst cramps of my life.

"And what exactly is it that I do for a living that's so horrible?" I ask. "I write stories about love. Yes, they have sex in them. So, what? Real life has sex and there's nothing offensive about two people in love expressing that love physically."

"I'm not sure that's the way the jury will think about it."

I've had enough. I stand up.

"This interview is not over," Mr. Mann says adamantly.

"You don't think I'm sympathetic, Mr. Mann? I am a newlywed whose fiancé was attacked and put into a coma by the same guy who attacked me. He had a gun and I had a pen. That's all. I could've died, but I didn't. I fought for my life then, just like I'm going to fight for my life if you decide to take this to trial. I write romance novels because I love the idea of love. I believe in true love and that's exactly what my husband and I have. We are destined to be together and I have no doubt in my mind that not only will he stand by me through this whole ordeal, he will also bring our baby to court with him. So, why don't you think about that? Why don't you think about what it will be like for you to put an innocent young mother on trial to defend herself against nonsense charges? Maybe your bosses won't look at that too keenly. Maybe they'll think that you should go out there and prosecute real criminals, not an innocent woman who should be at home taking care of her infant."

I push my chair back and walk toward the door.

"And now, gentlemen, you will have to excuse me, but I have to go have this baby."

CHAPTER 52 - ELLIE

*M*y cool and calm and everything is going to be okay attitude goes out of the window as soon as we get to the parking lot. That's when I realize that I'm about to have a baby and I freak out. To be honest, I've been terrified of giving birth. I know that many women look forward to the experience and want to feel every last bit of it. Well, not me. I'm really a wimp when it comes to pain. Especially, the kind of pain that I don't have much control over.

With all the drama surrounding my arrest and the wedding, I was able to put it out of my mind at least a little bit. Or at least, put it on the back burner. Well, not now. Now, Aiden is rushing me to the hospital as my stomach seizes in pangs of pain. I don't know what labor is going to be like, but I'm terrified. When I first got pregnant, I got a little Google-happy and read a lot of forum posts about what different women's experiences of labor were. Well, let me tell you, if you want to appease your anxiety about something, do not read about other people's experiences on an online forum. The issue is that women with good experiences of labor and delivery, you know, the ones that go smoothly and ones where nothing exciting happens do not take time out of their day to write their birth stories. The only ones that do are the ones with real stories to tell.

"I don't think I can do this," I say, tears running down my cheeks. "I'm so scared."

"It's going to be fine, Ellie. Everything will go well."

"Aiden, I have to tell you something," I whisper through the pain. "I don't want to feel anything. I know that this may make me sound like one of those not super enlightened mothers, but I just don't. I don't want to feel any pain. I just want it to be over."

"Well, if you want, you can get a C-section. Remember, you were telling me about that?"

I nod.

"There will still be pain afterward though," he says.

"Yes, I know, I know. But I'll be in recovery. It will be over."

"Ellie, this is your experience. I don't want you to suffer more than you have to. Whatever you want, honey. I just want both you and the baby to be fine."

I take a few deep breaths. Just knowing that this is an option is making me feel better. Okay, okay, if everything goes to shit and I don't want to do this anymore, I will have a C-section, I decide. It's my choice. I've read plenty about it. Planned C-sections take about twenty-five minutes and you don't feel a thing. They give you an epidural and you just lie there as they take the baby out. The recovery isn't bad either. You can even go home the next day if you want.

I take a deep breath as we walk into the hospital. They immediately place me into a wheel chair and wheel me into a room with my doctor and nursing staff. I realize that C-sections aren't for everyone and emergency ones can be hell, but somehow the idea of having one instead of facing an unknown number of hours in labor puts me at ease. If I want, this can all be over very quickly. And then, right before the doctor says anything, I make the decision.

———

TWO HOURS LATER, they wheel me out of the recovery room into my own room. My husband and our son are already there. The procedure took about twenty minutes, not counting the epidural and all the setup. Then they took me into the recovery room for forty-five minutes where they wrapped and unwrapped my legs and stomach, while I lay there unable to feel anything. Once they transfer me to the hospital bed, they hand me my son. I've seen and felt him on my chest in the operating room, but it's not the same thing as actually holding him now. I take him into my arms completely overwhelmed with emotions. Tears start to flow down my face.

"I love you, Ellie. You did so good," Aiden says. A little tear glistens in the corner of his eye as well.

"I love you, too," I whisper.

We stare at our baby, who is sleeping soundly in our arms.

"I have some news for you," Aiden says, without looking away from the baby. He's talking about the possible trial. I should have some sort of reaction, but I can't really elicit one. It's almost as if all of that is background noise now.

"Please don't tell me bad news right now."

"I won't," Aiden says.

Wait, did I hear that right? I look up at him. He shrugs.

"I won't tell you any bad news," he repeats himself.

"What do you mean?"

"Thurston called. They are dropping all charges."

"Really? Are you serious?" I gasp. "What made them change their minds?"

"Apparently, Mann's boss had it out for me. His family was family friends with Blake's family. He kept pushing them to file charges, but Mann only agreed to meet with you. The police told them that it was a very flimsy case, if that. Finally, after the sit-down, he just decided to not go ahead with them after all. They're dropping all charges."

"Oh my God!" I exclaim. A wave of relief sweeps over me. For a moment, it feels like I'm going to drop the baby.

"I'm so...happy," I whisper. "It's over. It's really over?"

"Yep."

"You hear that, Tristan? Mommy is not going to prison!" I say.

"So, you want to name him Tristan?" Aiden asks, looking at both of us lovingly. I shrug.

"We've talked about that name a lot, remember?"

"Oh, yes, of course. It's one of my favorites as well. I just wasn't sure it was your favorite."

I smile at him. "It is."

"Well, Tristan it is," he says, giving me a peck on the cheek. We had decided on the middle name a while ago. "Welcome to the world, Tristan Finn."

CHAPTER 53 - ELLIE

WHEN HE SURPRISES ME…

*T*o say that the days that follow are easy would be an understatement.

We are first-time parents, learning largely as we go. But we get through them. The days and nights all melt into one, but somehow one month passes and then another and Tristan keeps getting stronger and stronger.

He weighed eight pounds seven ounces at birth and didn't lose much in the coming weeks.

Much to my surprise, Aiden took time off from work and spent a lot of time with us. He offered to hire help, but I said we should wait on that for some time. Let's try to do this ourselves.

The best thing about the experience was how much Aiden helped out. Well, no, that's not the right word.

He's the father. Taking care of his child should not be called 'helping out.' But you know what I mean. He connected with Tristan right away and spent a lot of time with him.

He took on the responsibility of taking care of him most nights so I could get rest and sleep. After a while, we started splitting the night. I would take care of Tristan until around two a.m., feeding him once or twice as needed.

And he would take care of the rest of the night until around eight.

After a while, we got into a groove. Things started clicking and slowly but surely, Tristan started to eat more and more during the day and less and less at night.

"I have a surprise for you," Aiden says on the morning of Tristan's third month birthday.

It's early afternoon and the day has already been action-packed.

We've dressed Tristan up in a cute new outfit, took

pictures of him, fed him, he spit up all over his new outfit, we changed him into an old onesie, swaddled him, and put him in his swing for a nap.

"Oh, yeah?" I ask, sleepily. I got about eight hours of sleep last night, thanks to Aiden, but going to sleep so late has been taking a toll, nevertheless. I feel tired most days until well into the evening.

"Yep," he says. His eyes light up with that mysterious twinkle I haven't seen in a while. He sits down next to me on the couch.

"Is it a nanny? Because I might be more amenable to the idea of a night nurse right now," I say, stretching out in his lap.

"Yes, we can get a nanny or a night nurse, if you want," he says. "But that's not what this surprise is."

I look up at him. He pets my head and smiles at me.

He pauses for a moment, trying to formulate his words just right. My heart skips a beat. Oh, no, I think. What if it's something bad?

"Will you, Ellie Rhodes Black, sail away into the sunset with me?"

"What do you mean?" I ask, sitting up, a big wide smile spreading across my face.

"I want to take you and Tristan to the Caribbean where the sand is snow white and the water is crystal blue."

"For how long?" I ask.

"For however long you want. But I was thinking we can start with six months and go from there."

My heart skips a beat, again. This time in excitement.

"Really? We can do that? Really?"

Aiden nods and takes me into his arms. "We can do anything we want."

"When are we going?" I ask.

"The yacht is in Miami. The plane is ready to go now."

"Now?" I ask.

"Any time we want. I was thinking we'd leave tonight."

"But what about packing? We have to get everything together."

"The yacht has everything we need, for us and Tristan," he reassures me. "All you need is to pack some of your personal things and I'll get some of Tristan's."

"Are you packed already?" I ask. He nods.

I wrap my fingers firmly around his hand and bring it up to my lips.

I don't know what adventures await our little family in the future, but I know that I can't wait to find out.

After giving him a kiss on the lips, I get up and go pack a bag.

———

THANK you for reading BLACK LIMIT!

If you enjoyed Aiden and Ellie's story, I know that you will fall in love with Everly and Easton's dark romance. It's sensual, decadent and impossible to resist. **One-Click HOUSE OF YORK Now!**

They think that it's a game.

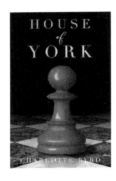

They think that everything is going to be okay.

I know the truth.

We have all lost our freedom a long time before we ever stepped foot in the House of York.

All but one of us will lose our lives.

Kidnapped, imprisoned, chained, and violated, I will do anything to escape.

But the only way out is to win the heart of the dark, demanding and powerful man.

I take a deep breath.

It's my turn to be shown.

Can I win this game?

Or will I lose my life along with my freedom?

One-Click HOUSE OF YORK Now!

————

Start reading HOUSE OF YORK Now!

Prologue - Easton

They are not supposed to be here. They are innocent and polite and sweet. Some of them may even be kind.

They think that they are here of their own free will.

They think that it's a game.

They think that everything is going to be okay.

I know the truth.

They are not here by accident. They were all carefully chosen.

Selected.

Identified.

Vetted.

Some are here because they are gorgeous, others because they will be good at bearing children. A few are lost souls who no one will ever look for.

But some, well, they are here because of their ability to fight.

Propensity to fight.

Willingness to fight.

Not everyone wants a fighter. Not everyone wants someone to resist their every move.

But some of them do. And these are the ones who will pay the most. And to find a girl who is both beautiful and a fighter? Well, that's everything, isn't it?

Of course, there will be the ones who fail. Most will fail at least once, but some will fail for good.

We call this game a competition to keep them pacified. Calm. Quiet.

But they had all lost their freedom a long time before they ever stepped foot on the island of York.

All but one will lose their lives.

————

Chapter 1 - Everly

Freedom is difficult to describe when you have it.

You go through life bogged down by life's little problems. You go to work at a job you don't particularly like.

You get paid way too little.

Thirty-four thousand dollars a year.

Your rent and monthly expenses are way too high.

Fifteen-hundred in rent and another three-hundred in student loan payments plus utilities. Of course, there's the myriad of other little but not inconsequential expenses.

The occasional lunch out.

Happy hour.

A movie once in a while.

Is this what it means to be an adult? I guess so.

After I graduated with my undergraduate degree in Psychology, I decided to work for a few years to save some money before going on to graduate school for my doctorate.

Of course, I wanted to work in the field. The only problem was that the only job I was qualified to do with just a bachelor's degree was to answer phones at a marriage therapist's office.

I scheduled appointments and dealt with the insurance companies. The job wasn't anything I ever wanted to do and I hated it.

I would sit in the freezer of an office with the zipper of my dress pants digging into my stomach, and I would feel sorry for myself. College was hard, but it was nothing in comparison to the grind of everyday life. School was broken up into semesters, and semesters into weeks, and weeks into classes and assignments. Even if a class was unbearable, as some requirements were, at least I knew when it would come to an end.

I can still remember the contempt that I felt for my job and my life, in general. Days became weeks and then months and years and everything in my life stayed the same. Clients called. Appointments were scheduled. Lunch was eaten. Money was made. Bills were paid.

But looking back now, trapped in this God-forsaken place, I would give anything to be there again.

To have that kind of freedom again.

"Number 19," a loud deep voice is piped in on the loud speaker. "It's your turn."

My heart sinks and I take a deep breath.

"I don't have all day," she says loudly.

I know what to do and I do it quickly. I pull off my tank top and take off my pajama bottoms. When the door opens, I'm completely nude. She looks me up and down.

I'm used to their glares. I don't know her name, I know her simply as C. There are twenty-six guards here. All called by different letters of the alphabet.

"Let's go," she says, leading me to the end of the hallway.

The ground is cold and wet under my bare feet. I'm ushered into a large shower room. Five others are there as well. We exchange knowing glances, but none of us dare to say a word.

We have exactly two minutes to wash our hair and bodies. After that, the water turns off automatically and the guards throw us a small hand towel to dry ourselves.

It wasn't that long ago when I worked at an office all day hating my job.

It wasn't that long ago that I thought that I didn't have any freedom.

Now, I know better.

Now, I know what real imprisonment is like.

Now, I know that the life that I hated so much before is one that I would do anything to get back to now.

After drying myself off, C leads me back to my cell. The walk back is even colder than before, but I appreciate being given the opportunity to clean myself.

"E will be in shortly," C says. "It's your turn to be shown."

My throat clenches up in fear.

To. Be. Shown.

What does that mean?

Chapter 2 - Everly

Being shown.

I've heard whispers about this, but none of the prisoners really know what's going to happen. The guards? They know. Of course, they know, but they aren't talking.

When C leaves, I put my pajamas back on and sit down on the bed. I wrap my hands around my knees, resting my head on top.

I wait.

A few minutes later, E comes in. Her hair is cut short, blunt at the edges, right by her chin. Her eyes are severe, without an inkling of compassion. Her skin is pale. Her bright red lips stand in stark contrast to the gray monotone uniform that all the guards down here wear.

Besides the bright red lips, she is not wearing a smudge of any other makeup.

She lays a garment bag and a big black makeup box on my bed.

"Strip," she says, sternly.

I do as she says. I know better than to resist. Once I'm completely nude, she looks me up and down. She brings her hand to my chest and bounces my left breast up and down, examining it for... something. I don't know what.

"Lie down on your back and open your legs."

I want to punch her. Kick her. Smash her in the face. But I remember what happened. Besides, I can't escape. The door locks automatically, and the only way out is through her fingerprints. Even if I could get out into the hallway, I wouldn't know where to go. And I can't very well drag a body with me to open the other doors.

I lie down on the bed as she says. I spread my legs.

She leans over me and again examines me.

"Stay just like that," she says and brings over her toolbox. My heart jumps into my throat, anticipating what she is about to do to me.

But I calm down a bit when I see her pull out a waxing kit. She warms the wax and carefully applies it to me using a wooden applicator stick.

A moment later, she puts on a strip of cloth and rips out my hair by the roots.

"Ouch!" I moan from the pain.

"Be quiet," she dismisses me.

The next strip she applies, I bite my tongue and keep quiet.

I've only been waxed once before and I ran out of there before the woman could finish. It was just too painful. But today, I don't have a choice.

She applies the hot strips and peels them off with expert precision. A few minutes later, I'm completely bald on top.

"Get on your knees."

"Why?"

"Do it."

I flip over.

"Stick your butt in the air and spread your legs."

I take a deep breath as she applies the hot wax to one of my ass cheeks. When she pulls the strip off, I can't help but yell out.

"Be quiet."

Trying to stay quiet as she finishes, I bury my face in the blanket and muffle my cries.

"Flip over."

"Is it over?"

She pushes me back to my back.

Then she spreads me wide open, exposing every last bit of me.

"Does it look like it's over?" she asks, pointing to the little hairs.

"You're taking all the hair?"

"Every last strand."

As soon as she wipes the hot wax inside of me, I realize that this is going to hurt way worse than any of the strips before. I grab onto the blankets with my hands and hold my breath.

"You're done. Get dressed, you big baby," E says. "Wait, before you do, lift up your arms."

I do as she says. She examines my armpits and then runs her eyes down my body, looking for stray hairs.

"Here," she says, handing me a razor and a bottle of liquid soap. "Go shave yourself."

I walk over to the small sink in the corner of my cell and do as she says. I run my hands down my legs and ask for permission to shave them. She nods. When I'm done, I let her examine me again. Finally, she gives me a nod of approval.

———

AFTER WASHING and drying her hands, she opens her makeup box. The box is so large that it has wheels like a suitcase. She gets out a big spotlight and shines it in my face. There is no mirror here, so I cannot see what she is doing as she starts to apply foundation to my face. All I see are the tools. Foundation brush. Concealer brush. Eyeshadow primer. Eyeshadow brush. Highlighter. After a few minutes, I lose track of everything that she's doing.

"So...how did you get this job?" I ask. Partly out of curiosity and partly out of boredom.

I haven't talked to anyone in days and life gets tedious that way.

But E ignores me.

"You're just not going to answer me?" I ask. She gives me a little shrug. Progress.

"Are you not allowed to talk?" I ask.

"Of course, I am," she says. Apparently, I have insulted her.

"So, why don't you answer me?"

She shrugs again.

"I applied for it."

"You applied for it?"

"Did I stutter?" she asks.

Now, it's my turn to shrug.

"So...you don't live here?" I ask.

I don't really know where here is, but I hope that she can help me figure it out.

"I just work here. I live on the mainland."

Wow. There's that word.

Mainland.

How long have I been here? I'm not sure exactly. But in all that time, I didn't realize that we were on an island.

Do you know what happens here? I want to ask. Do you know that we are all prisoners? You must. Of course, you do.

I want to ask, but I don't know who I'm talking to. She's a stranger. And just because she's a woman, doesn't mean that she is necessarily on my side. She is an employee, after all.

So, I decide to ask something else instead.

"So, what does E stand for?"

"It's just a letter."

"You don't have a regular name?"

"Not here."

"Why?"

"No one here has names. Privacy reasons."

I look straight into her eyes. Is she trying to tell me something? Reach out? Or is she just stating the facts?

"My name is Everly," I say. I need to make a connection, any way I can.

"No." E shakes her head. "Your name is Number 19. And you will never mention Everly again, if you know what's good for you."

It sounds like a threat, but it's not. More like sound advice from someone who has a little sympathy for me. At least, I hope so.

If she won't tell me anything about herself or this place, then maybe she will tell me something about what is about to happen.

"Why are you here?" I ask. "Why are you doing my makeup? Dressing me up?"

"Because that's my job."

"But what's it for?"

"You are going to be shown."

"What does that mean?"

"There will be a competition. A contest with judges. Only, it won't look like a contest. Everyone will want to be there. It's a privilege just to be chosen. You will all live in a big house together. Play. Have fun. But every few days, someone will leave."

The way she says the word 'leave' sends shivers through my body.

"What do you mean by leave?"

"There will only be one winner. And the winner will get to leave with her life."

"And…go home?"

"No." E shakes her head. "You will never go home. You will be his."

"Whose?"

"I've already said too much."

"That doesn't exactly sound like a contest you'd want to win," I say after a moment.

"It's not. But it's better than the alternative."

Can't wait to read more? **One-Click HOUSE OF YORK Now!**

———

Sign up for my **newsletter** to find out when I have new books!

You can also join my Facebook group, **Charlotte Byrd's Steamy Reads**, for exclusive giveaways and sneak peaks of future books.

I appreciate you sharing my books and telling your friends about them. Reviews help readers find my books! Please leave a review on your favorite site.

BOOKS BY CHARLOTTE BYRD

 ebt series (can be read in any order)

DEBT

OFFER

UNKNOWN

WEALTH

ABOUT CHARLOTTE BYRD

Charlotte Byrd is the bestselling author of many contemporary romance novels. She lives in Southern California with her husband, son, and a crazy toy Australian Shepherd. She loves books, hot weather and crystal blue waters.

Write her here:

charlotte@charlotte-byrd.com

Check out her books here:

www.charlotte-byrd.com

Connect with her here:

www.facebook.com/charlottebyrdbooks

Instagram: @charlottebyrdbooks

Twitter: @ByrdAuthor

Facebook Group: Charlotte Byrd's Steamy Reads

Newsletter

COPYRIGHT